TO RACE THROUGH A DARK CITY…

From a life filled with fast cars, stickball bats, and tommy guns, the man finally came to a place where he had met fear. Not the apprehension of the moment, not the uncertainty of death, but the knowledge, at the root of his soul, of something worth fearing. Even knowing that Dolczek's men were in the club, suspecting that they had followed him there that night, he had not been *afraid*. But now, with her in his arms, he knew the mobsters to be a threat to be dealt with sooner than later, and the shadows the real reason he should be running, maybe for the rest of his life.

But, not without her…

Around Eleven
A Novella of The Same Strange World
by Robert J. Schulenburg

Same Strange World Press
PO Box 43652
Tucson, AZ 85733-3652

Or Email us at:

info@samestrangeworld.com

Visit us on the web at:

www.samestrangeworld.com

ISBN-10: 0-6155260-2-0
ISBN-13: 978-0-6155260-2-7

Printed in the United States of America

Book Design by Robert J. Schulenburg

First Edition: August, 2011
10 9 8 7 6 5 4 3 2 1

DEDICATION

This book is dedicated to that specific woman
Whose smiles speak of sunrises
And whose mind does not see sunsets.

Around Eleven

❧ A Novella of The Same Strange World ❧

Robert J. Schulenburg

Table *of* Contents

Chapter One
The Bedroom

The headlights of passing cars became spotlights that played across the smooth surface of another place. As the light paused and hung for a moment in the corner of the room, a man stepped from the shadows and brought with him the hand, and arm, and body of a tall woman. Her platinum hair was piled high over a graceful neck and a delicately exposed back. Her gown fell in shimmering waves of silver that caught highlights from the mirror on my nightstand.

They danced to the rhythm the night played outside my window. They spun and swayed with the rattle of trucks. They caressed and held each other in time to the arguments of my upstairs neighbors. Finally, they waltzed to the sultry blues of a well-timed, out-of-work musician practicing his saxophone on a fire escape down the alley.

The couple was joined by the shadows of cats dancing across a chain link fence. The figures moved to their music in perfect ballroom form. The flashing lights of a tow truck caused a crowd of shadows to form on the dance floor, swirling around, with them.

And when the headlights finished their arcing sweep across my ceiling, touching the opposite wall as they were cut off by the limits of the window's edge, the man and the woman disappeared.

Chapter Two
The Dance Floor

The man and the woman stepped out onto the dance floor and began their swirling circuit through the crowd. At first, all he could think about was how radiant she looked. Their movements were without conflict or hesitation as they swayed and shifted together through the other dancers just outside the shifting spotlights.

Anyone watching would assume the couple had danced many such dances in many such clubs on many such nights. No one watching would have guessed how his heart had leaped earlier that evening when the man saw the woman for the first time by the bar, ordering that too-dry martini. No one watching would know how the light catching the silver lines of her gown had sent electricity to his brain and had seized his tongue. No one watching would have known her heartbreak, or the soothing balm his quite-shy smile had laid on her soul. No one watching would know that they had just met. No one watching would know that their trip across the dance floor was a means to avoid the distraction of crippling, awkward, conversation, as much as the result of the attraction that drew her hand to his hand, and his arm to her waist.

But even as he moved with her, danced with her, and was lost in her, the man became drawn outside of his reverie by the shadows outside the spotlight. It seemed to the man, as he looked over the woman's shoulder, that the walls of the club had been lost in a distance of glare, cigarette smoke, and shifting darkness. The woman's arm tightened around his middle. She had noticed too. Outside the spot that remained fixed on them (*and why did that damn light keep following them?* the woman wondered), she saw the shadows move at awkward angles, and the darkness overhead form irregular, alien, and altogether too-large depths to what should have been rafters and light riggings.

"I know," he whispered in her ear, "just keep moving."

They continued to dance, holding closer to each other as they went, suspecting only they were what was real, as the dark prowled and flashed around them.

The lights got brighter and the music dimmed. Then reality snapped the other way and they were dancing once again in shadows as the strains from the bandstand washed around them. Always though, the man and the woman stayed in their spotlight, holding each other.

At that moment, from the distance of a life filled with fast cars, stickball bats, and tommy guns, the man finally came to a place where he had met fear. Not the apprehension of the moment, not the uncertainty of death, but the knowledge, at the root of his soul, of something worth fearing. Even knowing that Dolczek's men were in the club, suspecting that they had followed him there that night, he had not been *afraid*. But now, with her in his arms, he knew the mobsters to be a threat to be dealt with sooner than later, but the shadows the real reason he should be running, maybe for the rest of his life.

But, not without her.

"We need to get out of here," he whispered into her hair.

"You think so?" Her steps remained light. He knew her voice was not mocking him, but offered general defiance of their circumstances.

"I have an idea, but I'll need your help." He spun them towards where the band faded in and out among the shadows outside the spotlight.

"Anything, let's just go."

Jack thought fast. He hated making things up as he went along, but it looked like it was going to be one of those nights where he didn't have a choice but to improvise. First order of business was to get her safe and out of the way. Then he'd need to make contact with someone who'd be able to help plot a course out of the city that could accommodate two passengers in the itinerary. He had some people in mind, but he was getting ahead of himself. *Improvise means start talking and stop when it starts to sound dumb. Stop planning or you could stand here all night not doing anything but making yourself a pretty target.*

"There's a back way out, under the bandstand. You take the trap door by the drummer's riser to the service duct and through to a supply room." He described briefly what to look for when she got there, then, "Okay, so remember, you'll have to go right and stay right when you get to the bottom of the ladder. Bear right at every fork. That's all you have to do. Stop at the fifth door. That's the supply room. Can you repeat the directions?"

Reciting in an almost sing-song voice, she replied, "Go right, stay right, stop at the fifth door." She managed to do this without rolling her eyes, for which he was grateful.

"Just remember that. You get lost and we may not find each other down there." He could see that she took him seriously. "I'll meet you there. Then we can make our way out."

"How does that involve my help?"

"There are some people following me. Like this weirdness isn't enough," he cocked his head to indicate the obvious, the swirling of shadows. "We'll need to make our way around them if we're going to get out. They'll be looking for a loser in a bad suit, not a couple out on the town, lost... with each other," he finished lamely.

"Right."

"You're okay? Coming with me I mean."

"We're going to need to talk," he could feel the half-smile as she pressed against him. "I may need to be asking you the same thing."

"Then it's decided. We shall Run Away together," he declared in mock triumph. Then he caught himself. "So to speak."

"Yes. Indeed."

"We can talk when I meet you in the storeroom. Right now let's just focus on getting out of the club and on to firmer ground." And with that he moved her to the edge of the floor and she slid from his arms and out of the light. He bowed slightly at her parting back, and then straightened as he saw her ducking behind the musicians. He dusted off his pants with his fingertips, and straightened his jacket with both hands. He still stood alone, in the spotlight, as the band wound down. The house lights came up as they concluded their set.

Strange. The shadows had gone. Reality had returned.

Which meant there was more normal terror to be dealt with. At least muscle and bullets were something he had experience with.

Better the devil you know...

Chapter Three
The Alley

It was nights like this that I would usually take a walk- late, warm, thick, and heavy. I didn't need any other excuses on nights like this, but I had crossed that fine line between needing fresh air and needing to clear my head that could prove the difference between sleeping at all, or letting the nightmares follow me into the morning.

Moot point, I conceded, directing my attention to the fact that the dreams seemed to be meeting me before I fell asleep now. What chance did I have of fighting off the night terrors and the damned shakes that lasted all day afterwards, if I found dreams waiting for me on my ceiling before closing my eyes?

Mom was right; I needed a shrink. Of course, for her, therapy meant simply finding a wife who made great pie. Proper interpretation of Mom's advice usually did me well. She'd say, *Find a woman who makes great pie and marry her before she can get any second thoughts.* I hear, *You need someone in your life who knows you inside and out and is* still *willing to talk to you.* Maybe I should make some phone calls in the morning. To Mom. Or that shrink.

I put my hands deep in the pockets of the windbreaker, pushing the corners of the unzipped jacket into arrows that pointed towards my sneakers. I dipped my chin so the bill of the baseball cap hid my face, and trudged like a cliché down the alley, through fog and around heaps of garbage.

I considered this new development in my nocturnal routine. The image, the dancing couple, that had to do with light, more than anything else. I hadn't noticed any shadows while they danced in their spotlight. Not my shadows, only theirs. For some reason, all the dark things on my ceiling held no terror for me, while the man and the woman were there. It was like the darkness had been pushed back by a bubble of light they pressed into the world. Pushed back to swirl and swarm, like a bubble had intruded into their normal invisible existence.

I clumphed through a gravel spill from some recent demolition work and ducked under a chain so I could turn down a driveway. I stopped dead.

The sky was an ambient orange-purple ceiling getting lower as the fog piled in. The universe went about its business of shrinking us into pockets of isolation as walls of mist came up the narrow streets and fell off of rooftops as it always did this close to the docks this time of night, this time of year. There were streetlights here and there on the actual streets, but I was making my way, by and large, following habitual routes lit only by the occasional back-lighted window pane from the apartments above, and the city's own banked glow.

I had come around the corner of a high wall that separated the alley I was walking down from the driveway that 'L'ed at a chain strung across the pavement at hip-height. The driveway came from the street to turn into some kind of loading dock. There was one harsh light mounted inside the small courtyard that spilled light just past its threshold, past the wall, and into the end of the driveway.

I stood with my back to the chain, my toes on the edge of the pool of light. Down the driveway was indistinct murk. To my right, was the darkness of the building facing the loading dock, not quite lit by the downcast spot in the dock's courtyard. Beside and behind me to either direction were narrowing distances that closed off any light as alley walls came together in the veil of night's gloom and poverty. My mouth hung open.

A man, across the yard, pulled a woman into the light. At first it parodied my earlier bedroom musings enough for me to close my eyes and shake my head to rattle something loose. When I opened them again, I could see that this was no set of dance partners. He pulled the woman roughly behind him by the wrist. He took three sloping strides into the center of the lot where a chair was set up in the middle of piles of crates that had been left out to be dealt with the next day. He twisted her arm, forcing her to stumble into the seat. She clung to its sides for support. I couldn't make out what was said over the not-quite-distant traffic. When the rumble of the passing traffic died, I realized that in fact, there was no sound from the couple whatsoever. No crunching of grit under his heavy stride. No scrape of the chair as the woman got settled.

Neither of them were in a position to see me, I figured. But she was turned more to face me, while the man moved more with his back to me as he circled around to a nearby crate.

The woman settled herself into the chair, cool with contempt. I have to be specific here. This was *the* woman. I hadn't stumbled upon some strange date-gone-wrong-and-about-to-end-badly after all. I wasn't sure if that would have been worse or better. I shook my head again, but nothing came loose.

The man was not *the* man though. I should be specific again. He was dressed in a suit, but looked like a gorilla- wide shoulders, hairy knuckles, and all. He was a brute. And he didn't like what she had just said.

He stepped up and slapped her hard across the mouth, just as a truck backfired a block away. A dog whimpered off to my right, and ran down the alley away from the noise. I looked back and saw that the woman was slumped back in the chair, blood trickling from her mouth in stark red contrast to her silver gown and pale skin.

Gorilla Boy went back to the crate he had been standing by and approached the woman again, carrying a length of rope that he used to tie her to the chair. He was muttering the whole time, the way bastards do when they want to justify hitting a woman. She stirred some, but she didn't struggle.

The cold fires came back into her eyes though, and I shivered despite the night's strange warmth.

When he was finished he stepped back and talked some more. She said nothing. She just stared at him, chin lifted, daring him again.

Her eyes flicked to the side. In that instant the big guy turned with her gaze, towards me.

And the light bulb exploded.

Chapter Four
The Bar

Inside the bar it was crowded and noisy. The swirl of people was almost as disconcerting as the swirl of shadows. Jake was as much on edge being without the girl, he'd have to remember to ask for her name, *idiot*, as he had been glimpsing the phantoms outside the spotlight on the dance floor. Electric attraction aside, he was worried for her, and wanted to be back with her again. She seemed worried enough when she took off for the bandstand that he figured she must have something going on in her head besides just ghosts and strangeness and an all-too-short slow dance. They'd have to talk, soon. He had to be honest with her about what he was about to do, what leaving town with him really meant, and the danger he was putting her in.

But there wasn't time for that right now. He leaned up against the bar, his left elbow on the rail, and looked down its length towards the barman. One guy in seven in this room was Dolczek's man. Jake felt exposed, vulnerable. Most of them knew him. Any of them could be aware of what was going down tonight.

The bartender was arguing with Tina and Luisa Martini. They were girls from the old neighborhood. Jake had known them since they were kids. And they still scared him. They were one or two years older than him, and always seemed to be just a little bit bigger and a little bit tougher. And always, they looked after their own interests. They were the biggest bullies, in some ways, that Jake had ever met.

Right now, they were cutting Mike, the bartender, deep with the sharpness of their tongues. Jake winced. He felt for the man.

From nowhere, but suddenly in his ear, "Just what the hell do you think you're looking at?"

Jake's heart stopped when it hit his throat. When he began to breathe again, he let out, "Jesus Christ, Cheese, what the hell are you thinking?"

The little man behind him had only brushed Jake's back with his empty shot glass, but it was just enough pressure on the back of the spine that the images of a snub nosed revolver being placed discretely between his shoulder blades filled Jake's consciousness. That, combined with the idea that he'd never see the girl again, (*Or learn her name, idiot. Why didn't you ask her what her name was?*) scared him as much as anything.

But Jake was relieved too. He hadn't expected to see Cheese tonight, and this made everything easier. He and Cheese went way back, and Cheese had a knack for finding anything, fast.

"A word of advice Jocko?"

Jake held his breath.

"Invest in a new suit. For Christ's sake man, have some dignity. That thing's better days are worse than its bad days used to be."

Jake took a moment to figure that out, and realized he'd been insulted. "I like this suit," Jake allowed himself a smile for the little squeak of a man. "Rumpled sure, but it moves with me. Pockets in all the right places. Black goes with anything. I thought you were working tonight."

"You'd need a crowbar to iron that thing. Yeah, the old man called me up late this afternoon and told me to come here. Didn't say why, just to come have a drink and take things easy, but it had to be here."

Jake thinned his lips in thought. "Well, I'm glad you're here. I could use your help."

Chapter Five
The Basement

A ladder flipped down and then slid out as it extended on inset runners, telescoping into the dark tunnel below the stage. The drummer looked down on her with a shrug. Not the craziest thing he'd seen in the club, not by far. An attractive woman in a fancy dress sneaking under his riser into some service duct he didn't even know about? Whatever, he picked up his sticks, saluted her retreating backside with a touch to the eyebrow, and got up from his stool to go out for a smoke.

Gloria backed out again and then went down, feet first, into the little hole that pulled out of the floor, glad the drummer had gone.

The funny thing about Monty's was the basements. That whole part of the city had been razed to the ground and rebuilt several times in the late 1800's following fire after fire and one or two riots. This close to the waterfront there weren't that many basements on the older buildings because of the water level making construction difficult for earlier work crews in the last century. So, as one of the last remaining old buildings Monty's Nightclub & Lounge had grown roots during the intermittent phases of construction that were pressed in around it and stripped away again over the years. A rabbit's warren of basements and bolt holes laced the ground at various levels immediately under and around the club, leading to rooms and cellars that often no longer had any connection with the new construction rising above them.

'New construction' nowadays meant old buildings crowded together near the prime real estate of the waterfront. Monty's was on the fringe, the gateway, of the district, and enjoyed easy access to downtown and the more affluent regions of The Crest, Las Villas, and The Towers. Just as Monty's enjoyed easy access to these neighborhoods, Monty's basements provided easy access for those neighbors Monty and his clientele were on easy terms with.

There was a basic set of service tunnels that must have once been part of a stable, because, Gloria thought as she worked her way down the passage she found herself in at the bottom of the ladder, it would easily accommodate two-team carriages. She had heard something about old basements being stables or loading docks for the older buildings that used to be warehouses, but the nature of cellars and those who dwelled in them was far removed from the world of balconies and grand staircases she was accustomed to.

Lighting was intermittent, provided by low wattage bulbs joined by wires cabled and cobbled along the ceiling. She moved down the black corridor slowly, not quite comfortable with walking boldly down the aisle of spotlights made by the lights. She continued, clinging to the shadows, until she got to the next junction, where she took a right. Three more forks and four ignored doors and she was fairly positive she was on the right track, but just as sure she would get lost retracing her steps.

She couldn't have traveled far, but in the winding of the corridors she was sure she was moving slow. She stepped up her pace as much as her high heels and poor lighting would allow, and came at last to the small, brown door she was told she'd find. The room was supposed to let into the back of a large storage room that had once had street access but now was backed by the wall of a non-descript tenement. It was supposed to be crowded with crates and old furniture, and the man in the rumpled suit with that damned half-smile *What was his name, anyway?* had said it was supposed to be comfortable.

But it was not supposed to be occupied.

The door was open all of five inches when the ham-sized fist wrapped itself around her wrist and she was pulled into the gloom beyond.

The man was huge, and she knew him. Built like a bull, Marcus was known as Mook by anyone that worked with him. He was one of Turino's enforcers. He was strong, loyal, and stupid. He was growling something under his breath as he dragged her into the room. The words didn't matter. She had been recognized.

He threw her into a chair that was set in the middle of that end of the room, under a pool of lamplight. The space was filled with boxes and crates, like her dance partner had said to expect. This was one of Monty's regular storerooms. One light bulb from overhead cast its shadows into the darker corners, and these shadows swam with an all-too-familiar kilter that made the edges of the world tilt when she looked at them too hard. She looked over her shoulder to where a table with another light overhead was set up on the far end of the room. Four figures looked up from their cards and one of them called over to Mook to ask what the hell he was doing at the door.

Mook blocked most of her view, since he was standing in front of her, and because of this, most of Gloria was blocked from the view of the men at the table. She thought she recognized Louie's hunched shoulders and Little Andy's white sport coat hovering over the table, but these were just guesses and her head was spinning from the shock of being yanked through the door.

She supported herself on the edge of the chair and drew herself into a more dignified position.

Mook moved to his left where he could lean menacingly against a crate and loom over her with a wicked, but still stupid, grin.

"'Da boss'll be happy with me today," the big fool chuckled in that low voice of his that always sounded to Gloria like drums being rolled down a hill. "He's been looking for you, you know."

"And if you bring me back to him after treating me like this, how happy will he be with you then?" She punctuated her question with a string of quick, harsh Italian syllables that initially left Mook unmoved despite their heat.

Before she could react enough to change the sneer on her face to an 'o' of shock, he was in front of her and his open hand had already passed her face. The pain from the monstrous slap registered a moment later as her vision cleared. Things went blurry again as the tears welled up. She tasted salt and metal from where her lip burst and bled into her mouth. She felt a trickle of blood crawl down her cheek from her nostril, also.

"That, little girl, is how much Mr. Turino gives a shit about how you is treated right now."

He turned away from her and went back to the crate he had been leaning against. He rummaged around and came back with a length of rope that he pulled off of some bundles inside of the crate. He muttered the whole time as he came back towards her, unrolling the rope between his thick fingers.

"Everyone's out looking for you, princess. There's a war about to come down now because of you. And what do you do? Show up right at the spot where you can do the most damage by showing up. And they call me stupid."

Her eyes fluttered the tears clear and she was able to glare at him again. She kept her mouth closed, eyes narrowed. Shadows continued to swim at the edges of the room, but her head was still ringing from the blow, and she couldn't be sure if she was suffering from the early effects of a concussion or if she was just loosing her grip on reality after the worst of bad days.

She didn't resist as he wound the cord around her. She was still trying to think straight. He finished and stepped back to admire his handy work, or just to ogle. She couldn't tell.

"Keep sitting still. We can't have you slipping away again."

The men at the table were beginning to take notice. A few had put down their cards. Little Andy was pushing back his chair. Between the crates between Mook and the poker game, shadows pulsed and pooled. One shadow, to her right, pulled away from the crate. Her eyes fixed on it.

Mook turned to follow her eyes, and turned his shoulders towards what she saw.

And the light bulb exploded.

Chapter Six
The Backstreets

The light flashed purple-white before going out, then the shadows rushed in. Not just filling into the loading docks, but up the alleyway from both sides. I bolted for the street and the pools of light I'd find there from islands of streetlamps and headlights from passing cars tracking between those nighttime archipelagoes.

I hit the pavement and turned right, downhill and into the wind coming up from the waterfront. I caught my breath and leaned against the first lamppost I came to. I looked around as much to get my bearings as to make sure I was alone in the yellow glow. No shadows. No phantoms in eveningwear. Just yellow haze and the creaks of distant ships on the wind.

I needed coffee. Sugar. Cream. And something covered in a non-dairy whipped topping. Maybe pie, but I was in no mood to be choosy. If a cheeseburger came off the grill with a cherry on top I'd probably take it in three bites.

As I walked I considered the case of Ed, the waiter at The Greasy Spoo. The Spoo was a waterfront fixture under any of several names, but most recently, The Greasy Spoo. Within hours of opening under new management a few years ago, the 'n' burned out in the bright neon sign out front. A dozen replacements met with snipped wires and well-aimed rocks from spirited members of the community who found a common nerve tickled by both the name, and the owner's persistent efforts to normalize what was basically a dive in a neighborhood that was basically meant for dives to be in. The owner finally admitted to losing the game and left the sign broken and the name changed. He even eventually got around to ordering new menus as his final concession of defeat.

But Ed had been there for at least ten years and two other owners. He came to town from upstate with a girl and a whole lot of plans. They weren't from upstate, but that's where they came from. The girl left him at least an owner ago. It wasn't that Ed had changed, or become a bad guy. Fact was, Ed hadn't changed at all. Not one bit. But his plans did.

And with his plans always changing, even when he was making them, he never moved. No motion, forward or back. He was a study in unfulfilled good intentions, and he carried a suitcase full of dreams.

Correction. One thing had changed since Celeste left him oh-those-many years ago. Ed's moved three times. Each time he takes a place farther and farther away from the Spoo. He walks home every night. After some days, after overtime, double shifts, or more, he gets home, goes to sleep, and turns around to do it again. He told me once that that's the only way to get to sleep some nights; he needs to be bone-tired when he hits the bed.

It's the plans, he said. They race in his mind, crowd his head, and don't go anywhere. He has to either work, or be with someone else, which isn't an option anymore, in order to distract himself from those damn plans, those ever-changing ideas.

Ed is afraid of being left alone, awake, with his old dreams. I was afraid of being alone, asleep, with these new ones.

Chapter Seven
The Storeroom

Cheese knew what had to be done. That's what Cheese did. Once Jake had laid it out and the little man nodded knowingly, Jake knew the fix was in.

The short fact was that if you wanted to get your hands on something Cheese was the man who knew who to talk to, when, and what to say so it didn't come back to bite you on the ass. Everybody knew that he was Dolczek's man, but Cheese seemed to be able to slip around to wherever he needed to be and talk to whoever he needed to talk to. Everybody liked Cheese, even those that owed him. More than a few people owed him favors. And everybody knew good business when they saw it. In this part of the city good business looked like a little man with a big smile and a pointy nose in a brown suit.

So Jake left the arrangements with Cheese and made his way to the foyer. Monty's was a maze above ground and below. The clientele liked it that way, nooks and crannies in the architecture made for easily arranged private meetings. Monty's was considered neutral territory, after a fashion. Its labyrinthine cellars and dining rooms, its vaulted ceilings and grand ballroom, they all made for a sanctuary of a sort.

All you had to do was get there. Monty's, despite its strict 'no gang war' policy, was squarely in Dolczek's territory. Nevertheless, the occasional man from Turino's, Diamante's, and even Lim's families could be found sipping drinks in dark corners. It paid to keep your eyes open at Monty's.

Jake always kept his eyes open. He made two Turinos on his way to the front, which meant there were more in the shadows. Even though his eyes were open, Jake was reluctant to probe too deeply into the darkness. The general gloom was bad enough without having to tempt fate by dwelling on the strange swirls of shadow that prowled the dance floor with him and that woman less than an hour ago.

He'd been moving carefully for the past three weeks. He'd be stepping even lighter tonight. He had planned on making his way out and around to the back where he'd get to the basements through a loading dock, but changed his mind as he entered the lobby. He spun left, and approached the coat room.

"Hey Gina. Saw your sisters inside." Jake smiled what he hoped was his best smile.

"No kidding, huh? Let me guess, you probably heard them first." Gina smiled back shyly. She was slim and taller than she seemed, but she drew herself in and away from men out of habit. Gina Martini was the youngest of the three, and the one that Jake felt most friendly towards. She was always just a little too shy and a little too innocent for Jake to want to try anything with her. She'd been working at Monty's for a few years, which is why the bar was at risk for Tina and Luisa's occasional invasions. She kept to herself though, which made Jake feel like he could trust her. She was from the old neighborhood, but wasn't a Turino.

Jake slipped his hand out of his pocket and laid it on the counter with the corner of a bill poking out towards the quiet, pretty girl. "I was wondering if you could do me a favor. I need to know if Tony D's inside, but I can't be seen looking for him. If you poked around and told him I was out here and wanted to talk…"

Gina shook her head.

"What? Can't do a guy a favor?" Jake's smile faltered slightly.

Gina's shy smile grew just the smallest of hairs, but she shook her head again. "No, Jake. Not for a guy who's lying. You've been in there long enough to know if Tony was around."

"Then help me out by disappearing for about five minutes? You don't want to know why."

She looked down at the paper corner poking out from under Jake's flat hand, and placed hers on top in a knowing kind of way. "Jake, we came from the same neighborhood. You've always been a gentleman, which never made sense. And, I've always hated it when you've lied, even though it usually made sense."

Jake cocked an eyebrow but she went on, raising the pitch and volume of her voice for the sake of the three or four small groups chatting in the foyer and the odd doorway. "That's sweet, honey, it *is* time for my break. You just watch the counter for me, I'll be right back."

Jake had the good sense to blush when she leaned over the counter and kissed him on the cheek. She lingered a moment and whispered, "You're gone, aren't you? I've heard things. Well good luck then. And Jake, if you're going for good, well, I guess I just wanted to say, that for the guys around here, you're pretty okay."

And then she hurried off, probably faster than she needed to.

Jake was left at the counter, the folded bill under his hand. Gina…? Could he have been so blind to have walked right past her for years and never suspected that…? He shook his head to clear the distraction. This was not what he needed right now.

What he did need right now, was to get around the counter and out of sight. He felt around in the corner behind the door that Gina had left open and the dim light over the counter went out, leaving the space in the coat room visible from the counter in as much darkness as if a black curtain had been drawn across the countertop.

Jake had had a lot of his life wasted at Monty's, but there were a few secrets divulged in his tour of duty for Dolczek that Monty couldn't avoid. The door under the bandstand wasn't the only way into the basements, just one of the more obvious.

Jake got down on his hands and knees and ran his left hand along the back wall of the coat room in the dark as coats and stoles brushed past his face and shoulders. He stopped when he came to a metal ventilation grate. He squared off, facing the grate, and hooked his fingers into the wire crosshatching. He lifted up. There was a shift and a click as the frame hit the real top of the groove the frame was set in, and then pulled back, letting the metal-framed grate fold down to the floor. He moved to the side and reached under and past the hinges that held the grate to that section of the polished wood floor.

He felt around until he found the hidden catch under the floor that made grate and wooden planks both fold down into a section of deeper darkness in the floor as big as the section in the wall the grate had set in, about two feet square each.

It was tight, but after he lowered the hinged floor and grate together so that they were vertical, Jake was able to swing into the darkness and plant his feet onto the ladder set into the side of the exposed shaft that he knew was there from past experience.

He hung back against the shaft wall and folded the floor up till the latch caught. He reached over the edge and brought the grate back up to be almost flush with the wall. He fumbled only slightly when he had to lift and pull the grate back into the frame grooves so it would sit flush, but he managed. From there all he had to do was climb down into the darkness.

Literally, not metaphorically, he thought, as he made his way rung by rung. Irony of Ironies, each step down brought him closer to the light, closer to escape. His time with Dolczek was over. There was no way to turn back, and he had no will to do so anymore. He'd spent most of the last three weeks wrestling with that decision and now his path was set.

He reached the passage floor and headed in the direction his memory led him, to the left and then the second right hand turning. He reached dim light by that second turn, but was in darkness again when he went down another side corridor, cloaked in shadows and recessed so that you'd only notice if your hand trailed the wall.

As he made his way towards the woman, towards the storeroom, he afforded himself one last thought about Gina. Now there was a puzzle. Jake didn't consider himself a stupid man, no stupider than any other man at any rate, when it came to women. But was it possible he'd had his head so turned around all these years that he hadn't noticed something going on with Gina?

She was from the old neighborhood, and he and she would take refuge together from her sisters and the other bullies whenever he was staying with his mother. He had always thought of her as a childhood friend, just one of the gang, before he noticed girls.

When he had gotten older, he noticed her of course; she was very pretty in her slim, shy way. But, she always seemed too… good, for him. Not that she was aloof or self-righteous; it was him- he was afraid of ruining the illusion of her quiet innocence.

So he just stayed away in the world he went into. College got him out of the neighborhood. His family brought him back. Nice people like Gina shouldn't have to be tagging along with him. She was who she was, and that was good. He was who he was. He knew better than to have any illusions.

But she had definitely been saying goodbye. That troubled him some. If Gina had somehow picked up on his situation with Dolczek, then lord only knew how hot the heat was out on the street tonight.

And instead of running hard, he was creeping through basements to find a woman whose name he didn't even know. Jake ran his hand down his face as he peeked around another corner. His life was much more messed up than he had figured an hour and a half ago. Thanks Gina. Thanks Mystery Woman.

Jake found the sheet of thickly painted plywood laid between two pipes that acted as a bolt hole out of the storeroom, assuming it wasn't blocked by crates or furniture. There was a shim nailed into the edge to give leverage in making space to slip in, but first Jake knelt and turned the shim on the nail to peek through the knothole underneath. Lights were on inside, and he could hear people. Jake frowned. There shouldn't be people, there should be person.

But, as Jake peered through the peephole, straining to hear what might be lurking beyond what he could see, he could tell there were at least five men in the room. None of them were particularly close at hand. No one was by the plywood door. At least no one making any noise was by the plywood door. Odds were that the people in there didn't even know that this door existed. Almost nobody did. Monty had shown Jake this panel himself years ago, and that spoke of its being not public knowledge. Monty kept his secrets close, and wouldn't have shown Jake if circumstances hadn't warranted it on that occasion. But that was another story.

Going inside was a chance Jake was going to have to take. He had to get into that room before the girl showed up.

With great care Jake made the partition move without making any noise on its wooden tracks. First a finger's width. Then a hand's breadth. Then a space big enough for his head. Then a shoulder. Then he was able to squeeze into the small vestibule formed by the high-stacked crates that hid the entrance from view from the rest of the room.

The boxes were stacked and cleverly arranged. If you looked through the right angles like a peephole, you could peer between the crates, assuming no one had moved any of them, you could get a good view to one side or the other of where the door opened into.

But, unless you were right on top of the wood panel door, you could not see it. The shadows of the crates, assuming the lights were turned on, fell across the gap in the wall when the door was open so that it was just one more black spot in a shadowy corner.

Nevertheless, Jake had to take care to get that door closed again; not wanting to take the chance that anyone wandering outside in the hallway would find the empty gap in the wall where the wood should have been. Even though it meant closing himself in with the unknown and uninvited.

Slowly again, his heart straining under his breathless effort, he eased the panel back into place with the occupied room at his back and only shadows to protect him. Ignoring the sweat that trickled down his neck like claws of ice, Jake moved as quietly as possible into a position to view the far end of the room where he heard voices in casual conversation.

It was a poker game. Five men sat at a table at the far end of the room under one of the two light bulb lamps strung from the ceiling in the miniature warehouse. By recognizing shadowed faces and distinctive body language Jake was able to identify at least four of the men at the table as 'Little Andy' Turino, Luigi 'Louie' Ricci, Franco Rossi, and Nancy Monteclaro.

Franco was a thug, just a soldier in Turino's mob. Little Andy however, was the son of one of Turino's first cousins and a Captain in that organization. Louie was Little Andy's Lieutenant, so it made sense that he'd be here if Little Andy was. Nancy was a ruthless killer with a hair trigger, probably made so by having to defend himself from the implications of his most horrible nickname. No one knew what Nancy's real name was, and no one remembered why people started calling him Nancy. Nancy never mentioned it or corrected anyone who called him Nancy, as long as they spoke with the most extreme courtesy and respect.

He didn't recognize the other man at the table, but figured it was another of Turino's men, considering the company he was keeping. This was bad. He had to figure out how to either get to the girl or get the room cleared before she showed up here and walked into a den of ruthless gangsters.

Jake pondered, ducking low as one of the players, the unknown man that Jake now recognized as Franco's Brother Stefan, turned in his chair and called over his shoulder, "Can you believe this guy, Mook? Thinks he can bluff his way past me?"

Jake froze. He felt like he died for just a second, his nerves finally hitting their maximum tensile threshold.

A low rumble came from behind the crates that Jake recognized after a moment as the chuckle of a very large man. Jake shifted his position slightly to get a bead on the other end of the room and saw that, indeed, a large, stupid man that he knew by the name of Mook was reclining in a chair that barely tolerated his weight.

Mook was under the other light in the room, near the door that he was presumably guarding, though his attention seemed more focused on the game at the table. Mook was a notorious figure in the territorial wars between the various organizations and families in the city. If he were smarter he could have been a Captain by now, but he was held back by a thickness of mentality that eventually used up his usefulness with various employers. He had worked for Dolczek for awhile before Jake had gone to college. The run-ins Jake had with him were legendary in the family. Mook had a talent for destruction that did not mesh with Jake's normal style of getting things done. He eventually moved on though, first to Lim, and then to Diamante, and eventually over to Turino, who apparently hadn't fired him yet.

Stefan was called back to the game but Jake kept his attention fixed on Mook. Lots of people hated Mook. Lots of people wanted him dead, mostly for good reasons, though some just on principle. He was formidable in a straight fight and worse in a dirty one. Jake would have to figure out a way to either start the dirty fight first, or, preferably, run away to catch up to the girl.

Jake was so rattled as he considered his options that he missed what Mook did not. A noise out in the hall had attracted Mook's attention and his head swung around even as his body lifted from the grateful chair. He moved with surprisingly delicate steps to the door and listened. He then took a step back and flexed his fingers ready as the door cracked open slightly.

With the swiftness of a man, like a bear, snatching fish from the river (Jake had heard rumors) Mook stuck his hand through the opening and came back with his prize, the hand, arm, then body, of the girl Jake was supposed to run away with.

He dragged her into the room, muttering something to himself that made her face register even greater shock. Mook tossed her into the chair he had been torturing earlier. He leaned against a nearby crate, still managing to loom over her, and she drew herself up defiantly.

They exchanged low, cool words that Jake could not follow from his distance. The poker game seemed, as he checked quickly, to be continuing, oblivious of the new arrival.

Jake turned back just in time to see Mook step up and slap the girl, hard, across the face. His jaw clenched. His fingers were twitching but he kept himself barely in check.

Mook turned away from her and went back to the crate he had been leaning against. He rummaged around and came back with a length of rope that he pulled off of some bundles inside of the crate. He muttered the whole time as he came back towards her, unrolling the rope between his thick fingers.

He growled something more to the girl as he went to work looping the rope around her. She didn't resist, first visibly unhinged by the force of the blow, then defiant again, glaring at the giant. He seemed to mutter something else. Jake heard movement at the other end of the room and assumed that the players were beginning to take notice.

When Mook slapped the girl, something snapped in Jake, something primal. He acted without thinking; he just started moving. With his pulse racing with rage, Jake worked around further through the maze of crates that formed the vestibule hiding the hidden wooden panel that led out into the back corridor. He wanted more than just a line of sight on Mook now. He wanted the ability to move. He knew that he also needed to cover the players at the card game. But he hadn't yet decided which group, the gorilla and the woman, or the boys at the table, that he would be able to cover, which group he was willing to turn his back to.

But then the decision was made for him. As he moved through the shadows, the woman's gaze shifted in his direction quickly enough, suddenly enough, that something got through Mook's thick skull and he reacted to it. He turned.

And Jake reacted too. He lifted his gun, the gun that was not in his hand a second ago, and he fired.

And the light bulb exploded.

That was his first target.

The flash was purple-white and it turned Mook into nothing more than a large black silhouette for a fraction of a second.

That was his second target.

The moment of blinding light was all he needed to drop the gorilla at that close range.

He could hear the woman struggling and was impressed that she didn't scream, or say anything for that matter. There was too much going on at the other end of the room. As Jake dived for Mook's body, looking for the gun that had to have been there somewhere, he hoped that the boys at the other end of the room would be busy enough for just a second in the confusion that he would be able to come up with a part two to his master plan.

But, as it often will, whether men have plans or not, Fate stepped in. The card game was done. The men had stood and were drawing their weapons. And, as Jake cleared the body, they began firing. Mook made more than enough cover for Jake laying on the ground as he patted the body down. He heard the first snap-whiz of zip gun bullets firing over his head in between the *cracks* of more bullets being fired.

He looked over his shoulder into the darkness and growled, "Tuck your chin. Duck."

He swept out savagely with his foot. He was hoping to catch a chair leg and was satisfied enough that he was able to hook one of the girl's calves. Her legs were fairly rigid, tucked under the chair. When she ducked her chin her body had gone stiff. He jerked back with his leg sending her up and over, backwards and away from him. She was now out of the way, even though he heard a *crack* that he hoped was the chair and not her skull on the concrete floor.

Jake continued to pat the body down as best he could, reaching over Mook's bulk blindly. It would only be less than a second before they stopped firing into the darkness madly, and his advantage would be lost as they inched their way towards him.

Fortunately, Mook was wearing a shoulder holster. And as his hands traced the leather straps down under his left armpit, Jake found a huge revolver, probably the only thing that could be found big enough that could accommodate the massive paws of the brute that would need to wield it.

It was like a small cannon in his hands, and he regretted the kickback before he had pulled the trigger for the first time, knowing that his aim wouldn't be great, but also knowing that anything that he hit would be minus a limb, at the least, if he managed to even so much as knick one of the targets. With that being said, the boys in the card game didn't stand a chance. He was in darkness, hidden behind a corpse the size of a whale. They were standing, in broad view, backlit by the only light in the room. They might as well have been ducks in a shooting gallery. Even as he managed with the recoil, having to readjust twice, he started to drop the boys one by one. He didn't care so much that he was making killing shots, as long as they were dropped on the ground.

When there were no more silhouettes, and there were no more shots being fired, he reached over to where the girl lay with his foot, found the chair, and whispered, "Are you okay? Are you alive?"

"Yes, I'm alive. And I'm almost out of this thing, too. The chair broke and I'm managing to get my arm free. There it is. Okay, hold on." He could hear her shifting as the chair toppled to the side.

More movement in the dark behind him, and then she was next to Jake on the ground. He slipped one arm around her waist and gave her a tight squeeze. That was all he could afford to give her. There were things that needed to be done.

So, he nudged her away with his hip and said, "We've got to get out of here. There's too much doing right now. We'll have to meet up with Cheese later." She began questioning him, but he quieted her. "Don't worry about it. Look, I'll explain later. Right now, let's get to the door."

And on elbows and knees, just in case the men at the other end of the room weren't entirely dead, the man and the woman made their way to where the door should have been. They crawled over splinters of wood and other shrapnel from the stray shots fired by the poker players, until they reached the door, and slid it open, letting in the faintest of light from the dim lamps down the hallway outside.

As they slipped out, he grabbed some of the higher boxes next to the door and brought them down to form a feeble barricade. And then from the other side on top of those. He doubted anybody had heard the shots from upstairs, but still, it would be better to slow down anyone who might be coming by to investigate, or any more of Turino's men who might be wandering the halls.

He patted himself down. *Damnit.* There were only two bullets left in the pocket where he kept his spare ammunition. The rest must have spilled out when he dove over the body or when he was crawling across the floor. This was not opportune.

He examined the walls near the door. Around the frame was lathe and plaster construction. He loaded the last two bullets into the derringer. Aiming carefully at a spot about four inches from the door post, he fired, making a large hole in the plaster and a neat circle in the slats of wood behind it. It didn't punch all the way through, but it did hit hard enough that he was able to knock out the board behind and get a grip with some fingers to yank free a clear space.

He poked his tie through the hole and grabbed the double backed loop of cloth as it teased out the hole inside the storeroom. He asked the girl, no wait, that wouldn't do anymore. He stopped what he was doing, turned to her, and asked, "What is your name, by the way?"

"Gloria."

"Gloria. I'm Jake. Pleased to meet you." Then he gave the two ends of the tie to Gloria and said, "Hold on to these."

He took the loop that was hanging through the hole on the inside of the wall, and slid the door closed enough that his arm through what was left of the opening could hook the post of the bolt with the loop of the tie. He pulled his arm free and told Gloria, "Okay, after I close it, start to pull it tight, slowly." He closed the door the rest of the way and she pulled the latch home. The bolt slid into the groove. And when she couldn't pull it any further, he pushed back on the door to make sure the bolt was all the way home. He told her to let go of one end and she pulled the rest of the tie through the hole, securing the door from the inside.

"Now if anybody comes through to check things out, this'll slow them down a bit. I hope. Confuse them at least. Maybe. Monty will be crazy about the hole in his wall, but it's not like he hasn't had any before. Alright, Gloria, plan B."

And they headed down the hallway, together.

As they walked, he considered his gun and its remaining bullet. He sheathed it with a flick that sent it home to its wrist holster, and then put on his tie. He wondered if he should just toss the gun. It was time for the killing to end. He had only one bullet left and could see no good use for it.

But still...

He noticed she was staring at him, so he straightened his suit and smiled his best smile. He was relieved when he could tell, even through the gloom, that she smiled back.

Chapter Eight
The Streetlight

I looked up from the sidewalk as I trudged and saw the man step from the darkness in front of me into the space in the street lit by a shop window whose lights were left on. His back was to me, and he moved almost casually.

Beyond him, past the light, a curtain was dropped on reality and darkness swam. I could make out what looked like a ladder. As the man turned to face me, shadows began to run up and down its length. I couldn't tell if they were falling from heaven to earth, or if they were descending down its rungs to... darker places.

The man looked in my direction, looked straight at me. My eyes met his. I could not tell if his met mine. But then the gun was in his hand. It was as if his wrist flicked and it was there. He raised it and there was a quick flash in the darkness in front of me.

A cool, sharp breeze whipped past my ear and then I was sitting on my hands like a crab. I had fallen backwards. I blinked, and it was as if the flash of the muzzle had erased him from the light in front of me. The shadows no longer swam behind the light. I had seen no sign of the woman.

I got up and dusted dirt off my backside. I adjusted my shoe, digging out a rock that was under the arch in my right sneaker. I brought the hood of my windbreaker up over my head, and started off down the street again, turning right down an alley, avoiding that particular patch of light. I did not know if I necessarily wanted to catch up with the man, now that he had fired a shot at me. I didn't even know if that was a rational thought. The fact that I was just shot at would probably sink in before I got my pie, but I kept heading for the Spoo, hoping shock would keep all such thoughts away someplace where my appetite wouldn't get spoiled.

Chapter Nine
The Ladder

The tunnel was black, and looked wet in the light of the little glow that came from overhead at the end of the passage. Shiny lines of light traced the edges of walls and floor as they walked down the shadowy length. There was a blackness beyond blackness around them, but nothing moved that shouldn't. Jake had checked, and he was sure she had too. They walked side by side, at a business pace, almost in step, shoulder to shoulder in the cramped space.

"So, how about that talk?"

Jake grimaced. "*That* talk'll have to wait. Thinking."

"Yeah, me too."

"Second thoughts?"

"No, just scary ones."

"Oh, that's good. No, wait a minute. That's bad."

"No worse than what we're dealing with now. You're not a real snappy conversationalist when you're thinking."

"Not my strong suit usually."

"What? Thinking or talking?"

He cocked an eyebrow at her. She had no idea what it meant, but he quirked the hint of a smile.

"Okay, fair enough," she shrugged. "What's the plan?"

He couldn't help smiling a full but thin smile over his set jaw this time. She had moxie, that's for sure. Not a lot of ladies you can throw that word around at, but she fit the bill. She still rubbed her forearms where the cords had rubbed red, but otherwise she walked next to him down the tunnel, in step with her eyes forward, chin high.

"Plan is, I find you a safe place to sit while I get some real information. No reason I can think of why Turino's men should have been downstairs. I wasn't aware of any meet, and they'd be far from home anyway. I need to make some calls and find out why they were here, then we'll talk and you can fill me in on why they're interested in you." He held up a hand to stop her open mouth. "Not now. Anyway, there's a diner I know where you'll never be expected to go." He eyed her up and down sideways in her evening gown. "Yeah, it'll be perfect."

He pulled up short of the end of the passage, just outside the edge of the light. They both seemed to hesitate as they considered it. "I'd better go first. To check it out." And he stepped into the shafts of streetlight that came through the cracks under a hatch set up in the wall. He wrestled briefly with some mechanism, and a ladder dropped down to allow him a leg up to the door. He opened it into the night, stuck his head outside, then went all the way out into the black-yellow hole onto the street.

Gloria waited. She hated waiting. She wished she had taken up smoking so she could wish she had a cigarette. She tapped her foot. At the edge of her hearing, back down the passage, her mind swore she heard something move, but she was already blinded by the light too much to see through the darkness at the other end of the tunnel where they had come from.

She turned back to the ladder in time to see Jake slide down, feet first, hands on the rails. He landed lightly, and stepped back out of the light to join her in the tunnel's gloom.

"Okay, all clear. Far as down the alley and what I could see of the street anyway. Here's what you do." He gave her directions to Greasy's, a diner by the waterfront where he knew she'd never be expected to be seen. He checked to make sure she knew the directions. Then he took her by the shoulders and kissed her full on the mouth. Quick and hot, then turned her to the ladder and watched her go up into the street. She didn't argue with word or gesture. She trusted him and she went without hesitation.

Jake watched her go, then stepped into the light to bring the ladder up and the hatch down.

"I did not just see that. There's no way in hell I just saw that."

The voice came like a ricochet down the passage, sharp, just missing Jake's heart. *How many beats can it skip in one night without stopping altogether?* Jake wondered in his conscious mind, the unimportant, stupid, part of his mind.

One layer lower in consciousness he thought, simultaneously, *Turn your head slowly, just enough to get a look.*

Deeper, *You already know what you're going to see. Tony D is behind you.*

Lower down still, *His voice is tight. He doesn't believe what he saw. He saw you with Gloria. He saw you kiss her. And he's angry.*

And at the core, in the reptilian center that told him to eat, sleep, and survive, *Lift your arm. Twitch your wrist. Curl your fingers. Grip the handle. Aim. Pull the trigger.*

And finally, as the faintest echo of reason, *There are shadows here. But you can shoot through a shadow.*

And there were shadows, he would realize later, for all of a split second in the corridor between him and Tony D. They swam, flew, made the darkness churn.

The holdout pistol slapped into his palm, propelled by the spring-loaded wrist sheath. The lighter Tony D held up to see by as he worked his way down the unfamiliar tunnel made a terribly perfect target. Jake fired just above the flame, just above Tony D's open mouth, open to keep talking through his disbelief. He hit Tony D square in the flicker-lit forehead. Tony D dropped, never having raised the gun he carried in his right hand. Jake lowered his arm as the body fell. Then, neither of them moved.

"Oh shit."   That was his voice, Jake thought, making the slow climb back to his conscious mind.

"Jake?" That was not his voice.

The new voice came from further down the corridor. Obviously Cheese's. Obviously shaken. That was bad. Cheese didn't do shaken.

"Yeah."

"Jake, did you just kill Dolczek's son?"

"Yeah."

"Oh shit."

"Yeah."

"Planning on killing anyone else right now?"

"No. Depends. What are you doing here?" Jake moved forward to start checking the body, but Cheese beat him to it. Dead was dead. Tony D, playboy son of the old man himself, and heir apparent to Dolczek's empire, was as dead as Jake was sure to be, if the old man ever caught up to him.

"Following you." Cheese knelt by the body and patted it down, rather than checking for vitals. He pulled two pistols, a money clip, a billfold, Tony's lighter, and a switchblade that he flicked in and out before dropping it down his jacket sleeve. "That was my job, remember? To catch up to you when I had what you wanted?" Cheese offered one of the side arms to Jake but he shook his head.

"No thanks."

"You can't just go around with that pop gun. You've got to carry something else for protection."

"No. I don't think so. I'm empty now. Spilled most of my spare ammo back in the storeroom and now I'm out. And I've been thinking, the whole point is that I'm getting out. I'm leaving. I'm putting it all behind me. I don't want word getting around that I'm packing heavy. I never have, it's not my style. I don't want people to start thinking it."

"Well, if that was your point," Cheese considered, looking down at the body of Tony D and then back up at his friend, "I think you've missed the point." He sucked air through his teeth, thinking, and started again.

"Jake my friend, you are a dead man."

"Yeah, I know," Jake said, considering the body he knelt over. He crossed himself without thinking, realizing he had unconsciously said a prayer for the man he'd just killed. He considered the gun in his hand, now useless without ammunition. He did this without looking, still considering Tony D's surprised face. Then he looked at the pistol. He looked back at the body, then drove the gun back into its wrist holster with his left hand.

"No, this is extra. This makes you Dead, and Sorry. I was just thinking before that you were just dead. Dolczek's out for you. This was not the night for you to go skipping town. There was a big meet for tonight, went bad. Not this one here. Before. No one really knows what the score was, but it went south, Dolczek's saying Turino didn't come through on his end of some big deal, and they were supposed to meet here to talk peace before all hell hit the streets tonight. Dolczek and Turino themselves are supposed to be on their way over for a face to face."

Jake groaned while Cheese continued. *So that's why Turino's men were in the club tonight. That's why Dolczek had so many men in the bar.* Just his luck to pick the one spot to get a drink and ask a few questions where all his former friends and oldest enemies were getting together to decide whether to kill each other or not. And this was the night he was going to make his move out of the family. And then he met Gloria. And then he had to rescue her. And, *oh god,* he broke up the meet before it happened.

"And then you broke up the meet before it happened. I can't decide if it was better that you left some of Turino's boys alive or that you went ahead and killed Mook. Nice job, by the way. We had a pool running on who'd be the one to do it. Figured that ox had it coming sooner or later. You made me thirty-five bucks. I had you down for gunshot in a month with an 'r' in it."

"You run in strange circles."

"I'm just trying to pay the bills. Anyway, problem is, those boys you left back there will be awake *and* moving around soon." He considered the sleeve of his jacket where he had slipped the knife a moment before.

"No."

"But Jake, they can finger you. And if Mr. Dolczek's already looking for you, he'll know you busted the meet. Or at least think it. He'll have to tell Turino, give him some explanation anyway, and then Turino will know you busted the meet, and then Dolczek's son'll be found dead... You're more than dead, pally. You're Dead and Sorry."

"Dolczek knows I'm on my way out."

"Word is he got your resignation letter." Cheese's smile widened, sharpening his nose. "I've always liked your style Jocko."

"I was hoping he wouldn't be getting it till I was gone and gone. I made bad time getting here; now everything's getting slowed up and mixed around. Was hoping I'd be out of here by now."

"You knew that wasn't going to happen."

"Hoping and knowing are mutually exclusive. You can do both."

"Too many big words." Cheese grimaced, considering. "You're dead, you know," reminding Jake of the obvious, again.

"Yeah."

"But, I got what you wanted. Pier 8, there's a freighter willing to take on passengers. Private room even. Light work, plus the money you'll owe me, and you're booked. Just get there by eleven. She sets sail tonight."

"Is there room for two? Plans are changing."

"I'm flattered, but we hardly know each other."

"No, not you, moron. There's this girl..."

"No, no, *no!*" Cheese practically squeaked with the emphasis of the last word. "You are *not* telling me a dame is getting involved in this. Did you kick a black cat through a mirror on the way over here tonight? Jocko, you're a madman. It'll be tough enough you getting out of the city without having to drag some skirt along behind you. Okay, okay, I can see there's no reasoning with you. Fine. Should be okay. I'll make a call and put the fix in with the captain. You'll owe me more money."

"Thank you. I'm good for it."

"No you're not. All right, let's figure this out. We've got a body to move."

Chapter Ten
The Rooftop

I kept moving towards The Spoo, but despite my growing need for coffee and pie I wasn't sure how quickly I wanted to get there. Turning back was still an option. The shadows would still be everywhere, no matter where I went. Home was as good as anyplace. And there was always the Sarah Lee I kept stashed in the back of the freezer.

As I walked I kept telling myself that I didn't really *need* to know whether or not the woman was still alive inside whatever drama was being played out in my mind. I didn't *need* to know what was going on. I didn't really *need* to know why I was shot at. *If* I was shot at.

I cut back and forth across a three block wide pace that still kept me moving eventually in the direction of the waterfront. The neighborhood crumbled as I got closer to the harbor. The streetlights were placed few and far between here, and most of them were out. Thank God. That gave me time to think.

Every time I saw the man and the woman, or even just the man, there were shadows. Not in the light, always behind it. As if they formed a curtain, a barricade. They were always on the other side of the light from me, never in my direct view. They were either glared indistinct by the intervening light or they danced unobscurred in my periphery. They swam. They crawled. They flapped their wings. They moved. They hunted. They watched. They were predators. But they also held territory. They had laid claim onto these people.

This was obvious now, from the way they moved, from the way they guarded. This was obvious in the way they always seemed to be looking at me because they were always looking at them.

Hindsight is a wonderful thing. Clarity comes with reflection. It makes you wonder why people don't put mirrors on the inside of their glasses.

That would never fly, I decided. Most folks really wouldn't want to get too good a look at what they'd have to see if all they had to look at was a mirror.

I looked up as a helicopter buzzed overhead, its searchlight probing into the alleyways like an anteater's tongue. It came over the lip of a two storey building, and the light hung onto the lip of the roof long enough for me to see them.

It happened faster than it takes to describe. First, the man walked up to the edge of the roof and looked down on me with his hands in his pockets. He made a gesture like flicking a cigarette, then looked over his shoulder where two other men appeared. One was small with a pointy nose, the other straight-shouldered with a clean suit. I began to back away, wondering if I was going to have guns drawn on me again.

They were struggling with something large wrapped in a tarp. The two men put it down at the edge of the rooftop. They all exchanged a few words. They seemed almost casual as they stood there, two of them smoking while the one man considered the bundled tarp at their feet. The man shrugged, and then the little man disappeared. The man bent to lift an end of the, yes, the body, and turned back to the roof. He didn't see the man in the clean suit pull the gun from his jacket.

Then the searchlight from the police chopper whipped away to the south to paint the side of an apartment building six blocks away, leaving me alone on the street with nothing above me but the fog.

Chapter Eleven
A Garden At Saint Simon's

Jake believed that trust was the dirtiest five-letter word in the English language. It is the purest word to be compared with its absence. As a word, and in typical experience, it has been stained, rusted, smeared, and forgotten. You would think that the word would appear in letters of white against a black, black sky. But for Jake they always seemed just a little bit brown, no matter how hard a voice scrubs them to be clean.

Except for Cheese. Jake knew he could rely on Cheese to get done what he needed done no matter what. It may not always come off the way they had planned, but Cheese *always* delivered.

* * *

It was several years ago when Cheese had brought Jake to the roof of the Basilica of St. Simon the Zealot. St. Simon's sat near the edge of Salvatore 'Diamond Sal'

Diamante's territory where it ran alongside Antonin Dolczek's. For this reason alone it was a good choice for where to have their meeting that night. It wasn't until Jake saw the friendly wave of Father Oliver as he and Cheese entered the foyer late that night that Jake understood that Cheese seemed to come here often, and his appearance here wasn't unexpected or unappreciated.

"That's odd," Jake murmured to himself as they took to the stairs behind the little door off to the side of the main entrance.

"What? He usually is up late polishing the silver and that sort of thing. He likes to keep the doors open as late as he can in case anyone wants to drop in for whatchamacallit, spiritual guidance."

"No, I get that, what I don't understand is how *you* know that."

"What? I have a life too, you know." Jake's little friend seemed almost comically diffident.

"But church? C'mon, I've known you forever and I know you'd spend your money and your time in the shadow of a smoky bar as soon as anywhere else."

"Yeah, but a man's got to have a place of his own too, and this is mine." And with that, Cheese stopped midway on the flight of stairs they were taking up the bell tower and turned the knob on an unobtrusive door that Jake had missed completely as they had climbed towards it.

The gloom of the belfry stairs was filled with a silver blue light from outside so that Jake had to blink as he stepped through after Cheese. When he blinked his vision clear again Jake gasped, and then chuckled at himself for gasping.

They had come out on a kind of patio- *a courtyard? No, a garden.*- filled with the whites, greys, greens, and delicate lapis blues of a clear, starry night. Benches were spread around the perimeter, as well as a mismatched assortment of sturdy but weathered chairs. All over the space, about forty by eighty feet Jake figured, were potted plants, shrubs, and flower boxes. At first it seemed cluttered, busy, but then Jake sensed a kind of organic reason to the way things had been arranged. He could tell where each place was like a sitting area unto itself, with its own view and its own temperament.

"This is incredible. How long have you known about this place?"

"I guess the Fathers've been setting up for as long as St. Simon's has been here. Probably started with one old guy pulling an old chair out here to take some air, then just sort of grew as more and more was brought up."

Jake turned slowly taking it all in. Walls surrounded on all sides, the backs to offices or storerooms, Jake figured. To the right from the door, towards the altar, the wall rose to the edge of a sloping roof that crested above the nave before breaking like a wave up and around the base of the Basilica's dome. To the left from the door to the bell tower the patio ended almost immediately, and was dominated by the belfry, which was only twenty feet or so above the patio here, but towered more than four stories above the street on the other side of the peak of the roofline. Its square, steepled pavilion, housing the three bells that called the community to mass and kept the time for the local business men, was just enough at odds with the baroque architecture of the Basilica's dome to make sense, here, in the garden, if not actually when viewed from the outside. It was like this hidden oasis was the real center of the building, a recessed courtyard built for who-only-knows what reason, left to gather the resident priests and give them their own sanctuary in a particularly hard neighborhood.

Jake's eyes traced the rooftops- the peaks and ridgelines of the Basilica and its attached structures. Winged figures in a variety of poses looked down on him and he grinned openly.

From outside, the rooftops of St. Simon's were distinguished in the city, maybe along the whole eastern seaboard, for its many quirks in architecture and design. It looked to be basically a church to the casual observer, dressed and shaped in some high-gothic or baroque design, but there were oddities that set it apart from your average cathedral.

There was a well-known legend, in the circles where such a legend would circulate, about the rivalry between two architects, Jameson and Sharpe, during the city's early years of industrialization and expansion. Moving from professional competition that had festered for years, to a passionate feud over the affections of a mysterious immigrant girl, these two men first exchanged public criticism, then shameful slander, culminating in violence in the form of several public fistfights and one reported exchange of gunfire. The whole thing came to a head near the turn of the century when Jameson was found dead, the woman was found to be missing, and Sharpe was left with a broken heart.

Jameson's last project, the construction of the Basilica of St. Simon the Zealot, could not be completed as planned. The only blueprints- all the working drafts Jameson referred to when overseeing the work site- were consumed in a fire that engulfed the back end of the construction site, including his on-site offices, the very night the man was found dead. His company was unable to cope with the loss of the man and his blueprints, and under pressure from the church to complete construction as quickly as possible, allowed themselves to be bought out of the project by Sharpe and his contractors.

Sharpe threw himself into his work. The Basilica itself was nearly completed at the time of the fire, but some of the structure had to be torn down and rebuilt. As a result, there were places where the church seemed to jig a little here and jag a little there as the two halves were grafted together. The front end remained dominated by the bell tower, in a vague homage to grand facades like Notre Dame in Paris, while the rear, over the altar, was capped with the grand expanse of St. Simon's great dome, in the manner of eastern churches such as the Hagia Sophia.

The collision of the two styles was subtle, but distinct. The ultimate expression of the art of two men came together in a clash of stone and timber. Columns, buttresses, vaults and rooflines vied for supremacy. In the end, on that hallowed ground, the contest became finished in a draw. Sharpe, the would-be victor, left town shortly after the church was consecrated.

Rumors spread that he had gone south. Some say he met up with the immigrant girl in another city. Some said he was on the run from the law. In any case, he was never heard from again, and any victory he could have realized professionally or morally following the death of his rival was never claimed.

Most people didn't have the sense of history or appreciation of architecture to put this whole passionate melodrama into perspective. Instead, they just looked up and wondered at the angels.

The rooftops of St. Simon's were not lined with gargoyles. They were in the original plans, but the order was cancelled under the project's new management.

Instead, a choir of angels were commissioned to ring the perimeter of the building's heights. In a variety of poses, not simply ranks of static soldiers at parade rest, the winged female forms crouched, danced, strode, watched, pondered, and stood ready. Each was a masterpiece unto themselves. Together, it was as if a part of the heavenly host had settled on the rooftops like a flock of birds taking their leisure during the course of a long migration.

If eagles flew in flocks... Jake thought.

And just to add one further sense of mystery to the whole thing, the architect had arranged the statues of the angels so that every other one was facing outward towards the street and the others were turned with their backs to the city, looking inward at each other.

This is what the people walking by noticed. Not the novelty of angels, white marble skin gleaming in the moonlight or shining in the day, but the oddity of half of the cohort having turned their backs on humanity, as if they had other things to consider.

But now it was clear to Jake, from where he stood in the garden. Half the army of angels looked out over the city, while a full half looked down here. Onto the church. Into the garden. And, as Jake followed their fixed gazes and tracked the rooflines and walls he could make out by the light of the stars, at the places where the two halves of the church met. The angels were arranged, definitely now, Jake realized, in such a way that they considered, watched, sat in judgment, guarded, prayed over, the garden, and the places where the church joined itself. They held vigil over the place where the final efforts of two passionate men finally touched, and ended.

Cheese caught Jake's gaze.

"I come up here to think sometimes."

"I can see why."

"Villains and angels, Jocko. A simplification of the world I can accept."

"Doesn't that put your own mortality into question? You've got to be on one side or the other, don't you?"

"Absolutely. And if it weren't for bad men like us, these lovely ladies would be out of a job. You know I love the ladies Jocko." Jake grimaced. He had never, in all the years he had known the little man, seen a lady give Cheese the time of day. "They need to know I'm out there just as much as I need to know they're up here looking out for me as I skulk around our shadowed world."

Jake pointed to the silent figures ringing the roof, indicating the stares as they looked down on the two men inside the secret garden. Cheese shrugged stubbornly. "They don't have to be looking *at* me to be looking out for me. Sheesh."

Jake decided it was time to change the subject. "When are they supposed to arrive?"

"What I've been told is that Luca and Paulie are coming to make the exchange. When I suggested coming here nobody had any particular objections."

"And why here again?"

Cheese shrugged. "Because I know it. Because there's only one way in or out. Because nobody else comes up here. At least none of the Fathers comes up while I've ever been up here. I think they know I come here to be by myself and they give me my space."

Jake studied his friend by the light of the moon. "What exactly do you come here to think about?"

Jake was genuinely curious, but Cheese was having none of it. "Nothing Jocko. Nothing worth mentioning.

It's just good to have your own place, know what I mean?"

"Yeah, I guess so." Jake thought briefly about his childhood and nodded. "Yeah, I got you."

They waited in silence near the middle of the garden, keeping an eye on the door. Jake took the two and a half foot long tube he had had slung over his shoulder and put it down carefully on a bench. After about ten minutes of quiet, the door opened slowly and Father Oliver poked his head out into the night.

He frowned slightly at Cheese, then nodded as if completing some silent benediction. He retreated into the darkness of the stairwell and was replaced in the doorway by Luca's shadowy form before Diamante's men finally emerged into the night.

Luca was big and dark, but clean. He wore a neat, black suit that was a shade darker than Cheese's brow jacket. A pencil thin mustache helped let you know if he was smiling or snarling. Tonight he was smiling.

"Jake, Cheese," he acknowledged both with a friendly nod as Paulie followed him into the garden. Both men were in their late thirties or early forties, and were two of Diamante's most trusted. Paulie, in comparison with Luca, was shorter and wider, but not fat. He moved with the lack of subtlety of a weightlifter, and didn't talk much. Paulie just nodded along with Luca as they walked towards the center of the garden.

"This is nice," Luca said, taking in the courtyard. "Quiet. We can do business up here without being interrupted?"

"For tonight," said Cheese, "It seemed like a good compromise, neutral, but I don't normally do business here. I would have picked someplace else if Mr. Dolczek would have let me, but he knew about the garden and said it should be here." He shrugged, then indicated they could all sit down on some benches that were set facing each other.

"Mr. Dolczek is very happy about this arrangement," Cheese began.

"As is Mr. Diamante. He sees splitting the profits in the gambling halls and sharing the protection money in this quarter as a good way to start doing business together."

"Mr. Dolczek thought it would be a good way to test how each of our organizations operate, work out any kinks in the system before we continue with merging our resources."

Jake let Cheese take the lead. Everyone present knew the score, but courtesy and formality had to be observed. Dolczek had been making concessions to Diamante for years, small ones, in the attempt to gather enough good will with the other organization that he could negotiate legitimate consolidation of their power bases. Dolczek controlled a sizable portion of territory, but Diamante had several lucrative enterprises in his own fiefdom. While Dolczek was not above all-out war, taking what he could and never letting go, it was not always his way. He preferred to have friends to having enemies, which added to his reputation for being fair, almost gentle, by the standards of their society.

But he wasn't soft. Antonin Dolczek ran one of the largest crime families in the city and that didn't come from being only nice. He'd avoid a fight if he could, but wouldn't back down from one if it came to his doorstep. Dolczek had been working on this deal for years in an effort to avoid unnecessary bloodshed as he expanded his empire, but even now Dolczek's men were arming for war in case it all went south.

So, while Jake's colleagues were going around armed to the teeth and waiting for trouble, Dolczek had put together this meeting to talk terms and make the final arrangements for operations to begin jointly in the district of the city that both families historically contested. They were all supposed to be unarmed, and were to bring gifts of substantial value to exchange as a token gesture of good will. Jake had made the arrangements for Dolczek in that department. Cheese worked out the details for the meeting.

And Dolczek had been serious about not being armed. He made Jake hand over the revolver he kept in his car, and then Jake had to watch as Cheese almost cried when he unloaded the three or four little pistols he had tucked away. Then Dolczek patted him down personally and removed the knives and another zip gun from his person. The men were left with strict orders to go in good faith and, obviously considering calling the whole thing off as he considered the arsenal Cheese had left on the table, finally bid them farewell and good luck.

"I think we're all on the same page here," Luca nodded. "But before we go any further, you did bring the gift, didn't you?" Luca's voice was easy, but cautious. Jake figured that he wanted to deal with as few of the details as possible, and would rather focus on the exchange, ending the meeting sooner than later.

Jake nodded and reached over to the nearby bench where he had left the tube. "We still have to hammer out the particulars of how we're going to do this thing."

"Of course, I was just wondering if you had the same problem we did."

"What's that," Cheese asked.

Luca shrugged. "Wasn't counting on the stairs. When we came in, the priest took us up to you when we asked if you were around." He knocked a thumb over his shoulder. "But ours is still downstairs in the car."

"We can pick it up when we're done." Jake wanted to get the particulars worked out and close the deal. He understood how Luca, known for his courage and daring under fire but not for his skill as a negotiator, would want to just do the exchange and shove off, but Jake wanted to make sure this was done right. Business first.

"Yeah, we figured that too, but then I got a look at this place and thought you'd really like to see it in the moonlight up here."

"What is it, some kind of statue or something?" Cheese's nose twitched slightly as his imagination began working.

"Yeah, marble, I think. Help Paulie bring it up and Jake and I can start work on the details."

"Sounds good. Go ahead Cheese. I'd rather get down to business."

The little man nodded and did his best to engage the ever-silent Paulie in conversation as they closed the wooden door to the stairway behind them as they made their way downstairs.

"Can I see it?" Luca asked, indicating the tube with the shoulder strap that Jake cradled in front of him.

"Sure, why not?" and handed it over.

Luca unscrewed the top of the tube and pulled free a roll of canvas. He carefully unrolled it and held it out in front of him. After a moment, he turned it end-to-end, as if he had been looking at it upside-down, but couldn't be sure.

"It's a Picasso. You'll have to frame it."

"Looks squiggly." He sounded dubious.

"Salvatore's no fool. He'll like it. Trust me."

"If you say so, Jake. Art's not my thing." Luca rolled it up quickly but carefully and put the painting back in the tube. He capped it, and then slung it over his shoulder, adjusting the strap so it fit comfortably. As Jake watched, Luca reached behind his back to shift the tube, and when he brought his hand around again it was holding a Colt revolver.

Jake sighed. He had hoped it wasn't going to be like this. He silently cursed himself for actually believing it wasn't going to be like this. Dolczek's optimism had set them up like lambs to the slaughter.

"This is more of my thing." Luca gestured with the gun for Jake to step back. Jake didn't.

"Don't make this hard, Jake."

"Is this your idea or Sal's? C'mon, tell me. Dolczek will want to know."

"It's been Mr. Diamante's intention the whole time to not go through with this harebrained consolidation, if that's what you mean. Quite frankly Jake, Mr. Diamante has had just about enough of that old polak kissing his ass and pretending to be Italian. He's put up with it for the past couple of years because it's been profitable to do so. But there's no way we'd go through with actually working with him. Sharing profits? Get serious. After tonight, Dolczek will know the score. Mr. Diamante's going to take that old man's empire apart piece by piece."

"You don't want to do this. Anything happens to me and Cheese and it will be bad for all of you."

"Mr. Diamante's got the situation well in hand, Jake. We know what we're doing."

"I really don't think you do."

"Enough, Jake." Luca cut him off and gestured with the gun towards the doorway. "You go first. No funny business. I've heard the stories about you. And you're still here and a lot of guys ain't, so I think at least some of them have got to be true. We'll take a little ride. Paulie should already have Cheese in the back of the car by now, or in the trunk. Either way. But don't worry Jake, I like you. I'll make it quick, in the end."

Jake almost believed that Luca was trying to show kindness with these words. *What kind of world am I living in?* he wondered, not for the first time. But out loud, he only said, "I don't think so."

Jake lunged. He counted on Luca's admission that he did not want to shoot Jake here on the roof to make him just a little indecisive, hopefully giving him the edge he needed.

From his sleeve Jake's stiletto slapped into his palm and Jake gripped it as he extended, driving the point towards Luca's chest. Jake hated guns. He was good with them, which made him hate them even more. No, Jake kept a gun in the car, and carried his knife, and hoped that that would be all he'd ever need for his protection.

Jake was fast, but Luca was faster, and smart. He jumped back and slapped at Jake's outstretched arm with his own free hand. This left Jake off balance, overextended, and with no momentum. He was effectively neutralized as Luca continued to back away.

"I'd heard about you Jake. There's a whole string of jokes going around about the guy who keeps bringing a knife to a gunfight. I'd ask you when you're going to learn, but I guess it doesn't matter now."

Luca pulled the hammer back. "This one's got a hair trigger Jake. Don't make me have to do this here. I'd rather we keep this civil."

Luca backed up so that Jake had a free line to the door, but no way to reach him with the stiletto he still held clenched in his right hand. He took up a position by the near wall, just under the belfry's pavilion.

Jake seethed. He had faced death before, but he had never been so helpless under its gaze. He bit back a string of bitter responses that would only make things worse. He was beginning to unravel mentally, pinned under the sight of Luca's gun.

He had to get calm. He had to think. He was tempted to pray. *Which makes sense, when you're about to be shot to death on the roof of a church.* Jake's gaze traveled up the wall to where the angels looked down on him. He hoped Cheese was right, that maybe they'd be grateful enough for not letting their life get boring that they might take pity on him someday.

As if to deny his hopes, a cloud passed over the moon, casting the garden in shadows.

And then...

And then...

One of the angels moved.

No, that can't be right.

Jake looked quickly back at Luca, then glanced again up at the belfry.

Time slowed and Jake took in several things in sequence.

There was definitely the sound of the flapping of wings.

A shadow detached itself from the ledge around the bell tower.

Two white feathers began drifting down from above.

The shadow lunged.

One, two, three, four, five pigeons took flight in all directions from the bell tower's pavilion.

Cheese fell on Luca.

Dropping from nearly twenty feet, Cheese hit the larger man like a sack of rocks. Jake dove to the side, but miraculously, Luca's gun did not go off. Luca was driven to the ground, absorbing Cheese's impact but still getting pinned under the little man and getting the wind knocked out of him.

Cheese rolled over quickly, and while still lying on top of Luca, grabbed the back of his head, lifted it slightly, and thumped it twice, hard, into the paving stones of the garden. Jake winced. Luca didn't move.

Cheese lay back, panting. Jake came over and picked up Luca's gun from where it lay next to the two prone men. "That, my friend, was amazing."

"No, Jocko," Cheese said, accepting Jake's offer to pull him up, "that, was stupid. There's a difference." Cheese looked at the stiletto, still clutched in Jake's hand. "Speaking of which, you know the one about the guy who brought a knife to a gunfight?"

"Yeah, heard it," Jake said, letting the knife slide back home.

"Gotta do something about that."

"I'll come up with something. Where's Paulie?"

Cheese gestured with his chin towards the belfry door, indicating that Paulie was either in the stairwell or somewhere below. He continued to dust himself off as he griped, "Can you believe that Jake? Where's the honor in these things anymore? Guy had a blackjack."

"What happened?"

Cheese shrugged. "So did I."

Not for the last time, Jake smiled and simply said, "Thank you."

"Yeah, whatever Jocko. C'mon, give me a hand with this guy."

Luca and Paulie, still alive, were left on Diamante's doorstep. Jake wondered why they had to be naked, but Cheese had insisted, and Jake wasn't about to start arguing with his friend about little things like that.

Chapter Twelve
The Canals

Jake was grateful that Cheese was with him to see this latest wrinkle through. The little man had retreated to the depths of Monty's basements to find something to cover the body with that might also make it easier to carry. Jake stayed, sitting vigil, with Tony D and the darkness.

He and Dolczek's son were never friends. They'd grown up in each other's company. They'd been intimately, painfully aware of each other's presence since Tony's mother died giving birth. He did not feel responsible for Tony, or what Tony had become, but Jake couldn't avoid the responsibility of what had happened tonight.

Jake had killed before. Death was nothing new to him. In his past, he'd seen too many friends die, and he'd taken his vengeance too many times. But he was empty now, in more ways than one. There'd finally been too much death and waste. Jake brooded, while he waited for

Cheese to return, over the fact that he couldn't stop the habit of decades. It was like death was taunting him, following him like a bad girlfriend, begging him to come back, that things would be different this time.

When his little friend had returned he was not alone. Jake rose quickly to his feet from where he was kneeling over Tony, and stood ready to greet the new arrival.

"Look who I found Jocko. Brought us some reinforcements."

"Shit Cheese, you weren't kidding. I don't know which of them looks worse either."

"Hi Marco, nice to see you too."

Marco was an established member of Dolczek's gang. He'd been made shortly after Jake had, and in a way, they'd grown up together in the organization. Marco was probably the one man Jake was closest to, next to Cheese.

Marco was a trim, handsome, always dapper man in his early thirties. He had a keen gaze behind often brooding eyes. Jake liked Marco because Marco could think. He'd rather be on a job with people that could think rather than people that could shoot.

Cheese quickly explained the situation to Marco so that Jake wouldn't have to. He told a story that was basically true, minus some incriminating details.

"So you've heard already that Jake is on his way out." Marco nodded as Cheese spun his yarn. "Tonight's the night. Bad night, I know. Too much going on, but Jake's been hiding out and doesn't appreciate how much of an inconvenience this is for us. You see Jake, Marco's been called to Monty's tonight too. I was just supposed to be in the bar as some sort of visible presence, but he was scheduled for that big meeting downstairs that I told you about; that one that never happened."

Jake kept his face impassive as Cheese talked around the shootout in the storeroom, making it seem that Jake was ignorant of most of the night's happenings. Jake suspected that he was, in fact, ignorant of most of the night's happenings, but was willing to let Cheese paint his picture with his own colors.

"Well, it didn't work out the way they'd planned and Marco's just as happy to be out of sight right now as we are. I let him know that Tony had seen you and followed you this far before he tried to drop you. It was self-defense Jake, Marco knows that, and he's willing to help us get the body out of here while there's still a bunch of confusion going on upstairs. This might just work to our advantage. Monty's sealing off the basement while Turino and everyone figures out the next thing to do. Monty doesn't want anyone down here anymore tonight. He's afraid of everyone starting to run around in his tunnels whacking each other and figures it might be bad for business. Good news is, he doesn't know we're already down here."

Jake cocked an eyebrow as if he was surprised at what Cheese was telling him. He constructed an expression on his face that told him that he was being filled in on matters that were distant and unconnected to his immediate concern of getting out of town.

Marco continued when Cheese wound down. "I had to say good bye Jake. We go back too far."

"I appreciate that, but from what I understand, this isn't something you want to get involved with tonight. There's bad business everywhere for everyone."

"No kidding. I can't say I was ever Tony's biggest fan, but this is some deep shit you've dug yourself into."

"Bastard had it coming," Cheese muttered. He was never a fan either.

"But it's still bad business. You're dead, you know."

"Yeah, I've heard that." Jake grimaced. He was getting tired of hearing it.

Marco dropped the bundle he was carrying and said, "Then we should get started while you're still moving, you freakin' headless chicken."

Cheese had scavenged, from somewhere, a heavy tarp and a bundle of cord they could use to tie up the body and make it easier to carry between them. While Jake and Marco managed Tony into position and laced him up inside his cocoon, Cheese outlined the plan.

"Best we can do on short notice, with no resources, no allies, and no way of moving without being seen, is to dump the body in the sewers and hope that it washes out to the bay. By the time the tides bring it back, with luck, the fishes will have done a number on it and no one will be able to identify the body. All the world has to know is that Tony D disappeared tonight. But nobody has to know for sure that he was killed or that we were involved."

The two men hoisted the limp bundle and Cheese walked along beside them, giving a little support, but mostly guiding them through the maze of corridors.

By the light of a flashlight that Cheese had produced from the mysterious confines of his suit jacket, the three made their way through tunnels and passages, eventually winding their way deeper under the streets until they had reached sewer level. Then it was simply a matter of hitting the right door to make the final passage into the canals beneath the city.

The sewer tunnels were extended under the city from the sea caves on the coast and in the harbor. Long ago, city planners decided that extending these caves and dredging new canals was the most cost-effective way to see to the city's sanitation. From the time of the Revolutionary War through the Civil War the caves, and later, the sewers, were the refuge of freedom fighters and escaped slaves. Later, other criminal elements took over and maintained the free flow of trade into the city, unencumbered by the bureaucratic constraints of tariffs or customs. The sewers had transformed from being an Underground Railroad into the Thieves' Highway.

But, while trade routes and storage space underground were as hotly contested as any piece of territory topside, passage was normally uncontested for the average errand boy or mug looking for a bolt hole. There was a sort of rough gentleman's agreement at play underground, in the dark, and a small peace usually reigned here less tentatively than in the world above.

Some channels ran narrow and swift, some deep and broad. There were some passages which always seemed dry, and some where the raised walkways were always flooded at least a little. Jake thought of this part of the city as some extreme extension of Monty's private labyrinth, but on a scale so massive and organic that it defied analysis. No map existed of the sewers, or the cave networks and basements that they connected to, and Jake doubted that one ever would. There was talk about dropping a subway line under much more of the city, and Jake couldn't decide if that was a good idea either. There was too much about the dark that made Jake uneasy at the best of times in this city. Traveling through these tunnels tonight, of all nights, Jake didn't envy the men whose job it would be to knock open more galleries and tunnels under the mazes and warrens and dens and hidden places under this fat, hot, greasy city.

Jake shook his head. No time for dwelling on things that won't matter. By eleven, either the city would have claimed him forever or let him go.

They stopped under one of a string of light bulbs strung by Monty to light the route out of one of his bolt holes. They'd only been traveling for about twenty minutes but already the weight of Tony D was taking its toll. There was a bright pool of light forcing the shadows back into the edges of their vision, and a steadily moving course of water rolling along next to them at the edge of the walkway.

Jake looked over his shoulder and the other two men nodded, and dropped their load unceremoniously on the stonework next to the canal. The shadows were swimming again, bending the curves of reality just slightly, brightening the light just slightly in contrast. Marco's eyes were hooded and betrayed no reaction to the swirling darkness. Cheese fidgeted and furtived, but also seemed unaffected by the strangeness that Jake had to concede only he could see.

"I guess this is far enough. Jake, if you want me to finish up that job for you I'll have to take off soon."

"Hold on a minute," Marco put a cigarette to his lips and made a gesture to Cheese that made the little man produce a lighter and toss it over. "There're some things you should know. Turino's on the warpath."

Cheese nodded. "Yeah, got that."

"But Lim is also up to something. Stay out of Chinatown and away from the waterfront if you can help it." Jake and Cheese exchanged quick glances but Marco didn't notice as he took another drag on his cigarette. "It's a bad night. I've no doubt that Dolczek is going to put a price on your head, Jake. Do yourself a favor Jake, keep looking over your shoulder till you know you're home free. Then look some more. Cheese, you have to keep your nose clean. When you get clear, you'd better go underground deep until things settle down. I know you're not a soldier, not like Jake and I. Do yourself a favor," he gestured with the lit cigarette, "and lay low."

"I know how to take care of myself, Marco. But I've never left a job undone and I've never left a fight unfinished. Don't worry though. Once Jake's good and gone I'll be like a ghost in this."

Jake just shrugged, cocking a smile. Cheese acknowledge it with a half-wave, and headed back the way they'd come.

Cheese seemed to walk right through a haze of shadows that moved like a school of fish swirling around a reef. They wove intricate patterns as they moved up and around his body, criss-crossing and weaving a delicate lattice of darkness around the small man as he stepped through their midst into the next pool of light down the corridor. Jake shuddered to himself. He had yet to feel the gauzy touch of those shadows and did not think he would welcome it. No, he was content to stay in the light rather than mingle with those unknown legions.

Oblivious to the company Jake saw him in, Cheese took the right hand turn at the lit intersection and was gone from view. As he left, the shadows seemed to thicken, though they remained just as insubstantial, and just as difficult to look at directly.

Marco was as ignorant of the wraiths as Cheese, but he was not taking notice of much anyway. His eyes were hooded still and his brow was slightly knit as he considered something deep in the back of his mind.

It wasn't unusual for Marco to be lost in thought. He was a thinker by nature. If Jake wanted to be critical, he'd use the word 'plotter'. Marco always considered all the angles. Like Cheese, but in a quieter way, keeping his ideas to himself until they would be useful for other people to comment on.

The shadows were swimming furiously at the edge of Jake's vision. Marco was too busy considering his lit cigarette to notice. Even after he turned to look after Cheese as his footsteps receded down the corridor, he did so in a way that was so distracted that Jake doubted much was registering.

The shadows continued their dance, swarming and throbbing in their weird middle distance beyond the boundaries of the light. Jake was on edge, and didn't want to be. He was getting tired of how they always seemed to be at his back when things got dangerous. Their inherent distraction was frustrating. He had enough to keep his mind occupied with an impending mob war between his greatest rivals and the men he had just betrayed, to want to have to worry about the doings of black phantoms that danced on the edge of his reason.

He turned his back to Marco, and, he hoped, to them, as he put his focus on Tony's wrapped body and the edge of the watercourse.

"You ready to get this over so we can get going too?"

"Yeah."

Instinct told him to freeze. A splinter of a moment later he processed the sound of a hammer being locked back on a handgun. Marco's handgun.

"I told you that you should keep an eye out over your shoulder Jake. Hands on the back of your head. Slowly."

"Marco..." Jake's voice showed how wounded he felt. Marco, besides Cheese, was the closest thing he had to what could be called a friend. They'd run together since Marco'd been made, since before then. Now here he was, unarmed, in a sewer, with a gun at his back, and without a friend in sight.

"Don't turn around Jake. No sudden moves."

"I just want to talk. I think we should just talk."

"We'll do that. I want you to know good and well what's happening and what's going to happen."

"Let me turn around," Jake tried again. "I just want to talk. I'm empty."

"And I'm not taking any chances. You're too good Jake. There are too many stories about you."

"Lies, mostly."

"It's the 'some' part of mostly that I'm worried about. Do you know what's happened since you disappeared?"

"Couldn't be much."

"You'd be surprised. Lenny's dead."

"Yes." Jake had heard, and his voice was heavy.

"Now Tony's dead. In a minute, you'll be dead."

"Doesn't have to happen. You don't have to do this Marco."

"Yeah, I do. See, when Lenny went down and you disappeared, the old man started going to me to get things done. Tony was tied up and, I don't know, it was like Big D was almost lonely. I've been pulled up in the past couple of weeks. I was set to become Tony's lieutenant. Life has been pretty sweet."

"Well, that's great. Sounds like you're on the fast track. But you won't gain anything by knocking me off."

"There's everything to gain." Marco paused and Jake suffered the weight of the dramatic moment.

"He needs an heir," Jake finished for him.

Nonplussed, Marco rolled on. "Pretty quick on the uptake, Jake. That time in college must've paid off."

"Not like you'd think."

"Whatever. But you've got the picture. The old man's already been showing me more attention in the last few weeks. I've been in on meetings, lined up some jobs. I've proven myself, and now it's really going to be my time. Imagine, you- gone. Tony- gone. Even old Lenny-gone. And here I come, bringing you in as a trophy, the source of his recent grief, and the murderer of his only son."

"It won't work the way you're thinking Marco."

"The hell it won't."

"It won't. Dolczek won't be happy to see me dead, or know that you're the man to pull the trigger. I'm his nephew."

"I don't buy it. The old man ain't got no nephew. Ain't got no family except Tony D."

"And my mother, his sister, who married Italian. How do you think Dolczek got in so tight with Turino's grandfather in the old days?"

"You're telling me that you're a Turino now too?"

"No, my dad was just a guy from the neighborhood who ran with Turino's boys way back. We're not part of the family. Especially not now." Jake had meant 'now' as in 'now that Dolczek has set up his own empire. But, Marco grunted as if he understood something else.

"So that's it. That's why you've been hanging around him what seems like forever. I thought you had come in young."

"It's not something we talk about."

"I'm going to have to thank you for that Jake. That really is a lot to think about. But would the old man be put out that you've been clipped after he finds out about his son? Hmmm."

Marco really seemed to consider it, and Jake's mind raced with desperate hope.

Then crashed.

"No, I don't think so. Especially not after today. You weren't there Jake. And, I suppose you should have been, if you hadn't taken off already. It was a real big deal. This thing with Turino was going to be big. But then it fell through. Turino didn't deliver the goods and claimed it wasn't his fault. Tony D was fit to be tied, and I can't blame him. Dolczek though," Marco had almost been audibly grinning, but now his voice grew reverent, "Dolczek just got cold. Quiet. The way he can. No Jake, I'm pretty sure he wants blood, or will if he doesn't already. I think yours'll do."

"Marco…"

The gunman at his back was on a roll, albeit a melodramatic one. *Fine,* Jake thought, *keep talking. Give me time to think.*

"I'm thinking that there're enough rumors flying around to tie you into some of what's happened today. I mean, c'mon Jake, you disappear, it all hits the fan today, Cheese didn't say, but I'm thinking you were involved in that mess under Monty's, and I *know* that you shot Tony D. You're in deep."

"Don't you think Cheese will put this all together? You offing me? Dolczek might not care, or maybe he will, that you put me down. But Cheese could still finger you to the cops. C'mon Marco. You know I'm on my way out. You don't have to do this." Jake kept talking, but was aware that, even to himself, he was sounding desperate.

Marco seemed to consider this for a moment. Then came back with, "Nah, we'll do this my way. A body will go a lot farther with the old man, especially if I'm bringing his son back to him in the same load. Besides, Cheese won't say anything to Dolczek because he would be tipping his hand about his part in helping to get you out of town, not to mention him helping to try to dump Tony D's body."

"No," Marco declared with finality, "don't worry Jake, that little rat won't be any problem. He's practically already dealt with. All the bases are covered."

The first shot flew across the bridge of Marco's nose. He had maybe just enough time for that to register before shots two, three, and four slammed into the ribs on his right side and he began leaking oxygen and blood. Shot five clipped his hip, spinning him around. But, he only had the briefest moment of sensation of the movement, force, and pain, because shot six tore his head apart.

Six peals of thunder, six lightning flashes from an unseen muzzle, and one wet heavy thump played across the space behind Jake, filling the causeway and crowding his senses.

The echoes of ricochets down the stone tunnels pinged counterpoint to the dripping pipes. Jake held his pose for three heartbeats before acknowledging that he was not only alive, but un-shot. He lowered his arms slowly, straightened his rumpled suit jacket, and turned.

Cheese stepped out of the shadows of the tunnel. He moved unhurriedly to the body, tossing his gun, Tony D's gun, into the canal as he approached the body. He started patting it down, and true to form, he looted Marco's pistol, another billfold, a spare clip, and a silk handkerchief before letting out a small 'ah ha' and raising his true prize.

"Bum stole my lighter."

"Cheese?"

"Yeah."

"Cheese, did you just kill Marco?"

"Yeah."

Jake realized how the conversation was becoming a parody of the moments after Tony D's death. He didn't want to go down that road again, so he nodded and simply said, "Good."

It occurred to Jake that Cheese's lighter was actually the lighter that Cheese had lifted off of Tony D. He decided it wasn't worth pursuing the matter.

"You couldn't have said anything? Like 'Duck!' or given me some kind of warning or something?"

Cheese finished inspecting Marco's handgun and adjusting his new loot in his various pockets. He squared his shoulders and looked his friend square in the eyes.

"Honestly Jocko, do I look like the kind of idiot who gives a guy any warning before shooting him? Leave that for the other guys, whatchacalum, heroes.. I'd rather live through my ambush than die giving a speech."

In all their years of friendship, Jake couldn't remember a time when he had ever seen Cheese shoot anyone down like that. They'd been in brawls. They'd shot out their fair share of windows together. But this was different, Jake realized. This was, well, murder. He'd never seen that in Cheese before. Jake hoped he'd never see it again.

"I didn't know you could shoot like that."

Cheese shrugged.

"Thank you."

Cheese sighed deeply. "Don't thank me Jocko. Every time you thank me there winds up being another body to deal with later."

Chapter Thirteen
An Old Man's Study

Shadows sunk their teeth into the lawns outside as an old man sat behind his desk, alone, in his study. His back was to the french door so he could not see the graying sky. Even though it was growing steadily dim, he did not turn the lights on. The grandfather clock tick-tocked away the time, the seconds hand speeding around its course. The white face of the clock was like a full moon in the shadows of the study.

* * *

Sparks from the campfire flew up into the night to mix with the stars that danced around the full moon.

"You did good today Jake. You did real good. You're a fine shot. Brought down all of those squirrels." The older man beamed with pride at the boy to rival the light of the fire and the moon both.

The boy poked the fire with a stick, driving more of the fire's ghosts into the night. "Why do you call me Jake, Uncle Tony? Why don't you call me Giovanni, or Johnny like momma does?"

The older man smiled and pursed his lips. "For two reasons. First, because we are in America. I've made this my home. You were born to it. We are to be Americans in America." Jake tried not to laugh at the words spoken through the filter of the thick polish accent. He managed to reduce the amusing insight to a quiet, half-smirk, subtle for his age.

"Second, I call you Jake because I can have no favorites. Antonio Giovanni Garibaldi cannot be my nephew. But, I will always find time to spend with you, Jake."

He looked up at the sky and then back at the boy. "This has been a good trip, eh? We have that." He ruffled the boy's hair. "Why do I need to call you Johnny, eh? As long as you're visiting, as long as you stay with me, you'll always be Jake."

* * *

The tips of the candle flames waved like palm trees in a hurricane as a string of Polish was interrupted by Italian swear words, which themselves were punctuated by the old man's fist pounding the table again and again for emphasis.

The young man at the end of the table chewed quietly, his expression blank. The early adolescent in-between them smiled and looked from one to the other in anticipation of what would come next. The tirade finally ground down to English again.

"This is final Jake," the old man stabbed a finger at the youth from across the table. "You're going to college. You're too smart for this," he gestured vaguely around the room in order to encompass a lifestyle, "and you're too good for it."

The young man stopped chewing his food and put his utensils down. He looked at his uncle like he was trying to study him from far away.

"I know what you're thinking. You're thinking I'm pushing you away." This time Dolczek stabbed his fork at the young man, his nephew. "But I'm not pushing you away, I'm trying to push you towards something. Do you think this is what I want for you?" He gestured again at the universe with an upward twirl of the fork.

"What is that supposed to mean? How are you supposed to expect me to answer that question? You want this for someone." The young man, Jake, glanced at the youth halfway between him and his uncle and concluded, "There's something here worth having."

Dolczek couldn't keep his voice from rising. "I've cared for you. I've cared for your mother, *and* I'm making sure you get the best education. I've lined your pockets and made sure you had everything that you need.

The young man's tone was icy now. His eyes were black as flint. There was no trace of that smile that defined him. "I'm not talking about the money."

Dolczek shuddered slightly at the chill cast down the table at him but continued with resolve. "Anthony is my son, and he will get what's coming to him." The youth's grin broadened. "You are my nephew, who I love, and you will get what you deserve also. And that includes going away to college, getting out, not having to be part of this. You will have that better life. *You* will take care of you mother. You don't have to be in here, with us, my son and I. We are hard men. We have to be because we do hard things."

"I can…"

"I know you can, but that doesn't mean you *should*. That's why you're going to school. Accept it."

He knew Jake would come back. But it still hurt him when the young man, all of seventeen, stood up, folding his napkin- cleanly, crisply- and put it back on the table next to his plate. He turned on his toe, and left the house

* * *

The lights in the upstairs hall had never seemed bright enough to Antonin Dolczek. He was always disturbed by the way the shadows forever seemed to be cast, long and thin, in front of him, never behind him, like proper light should throw darkness. He walked along the shadow lines in the darkness from the staircase, past the bedrooms, to the study at the front of the house. He could already hear the boys talking.

He could hear them talking as the clock kept ticking and the pendulum swung in time. They weren't fighting. They weren't even bickering. Jake's voice came, as quiet, as simple, as direct as always, holding emotion away as he needed to. Which was always a sure sign he was on edge. A tell that most people never observed.

Little Anthony, on the other hand, was not displaying his normal, smooth, seductive tone of speech. The old man had to admit that he sounded like he was braying, like a donkey. It sounded something like this.

"It was my crew that took over the First National that day."

"I've heard." Jake was not smiling.

"Yeah, you heard that it was taken over, but you never heard that it was my crew. We got out of there *clean.*"

"I heard there were… a couple of people shot."

"None of my guys. And, nobody died. So no murder rap."

"So far."

"Yeah, so far. Like I said."

"And what was the take on that job?"

"Don't worry about the take on that. The important thing is that they know we're out there, that they know we're in charge."

"And?" Jake prompted quietly.

"And? *And?* And, we're moving into The Heights. *And*, more and more blocks in the waterfront are belonging to us. *And…*"

Antonin Dolczek tuned out the rest of the *And*s. Each one was like the hiccup of a bucking mule. He could take it no longer, so he walked in and made his presence known.

"Good evening boys. Jake, good to see you."

Jake nodded out of courtesy, keeping his distance, out of courtesy.

"Your mother, she is doing well tonight?"

"Yes, I just left her. She made the best ziti."

"I know. It is wonderful."

"I'll bring you back some, next time I visit."

"That would be nice. She does not come to visit me, like she used to."

"No, she prefers the old neighborhood. You know that."

"Yes. I remember."

Dolczek motioned the boys to chairs opposite the desk so he could take his point in front of the big window. He folded his hands in front of him in a position of prayer, looked up, laid his palms flat on the table, cleared his throat, and said, "I wanted you both to be here so I could talk with you both directly. I have plans that I need you for. And I did not want to talk to one before the other, out of respect for both of you. My son, whom I love, Jake, is coming into his own. He is a Captain in his own right. But I need your help. There are things you know that his experience has not yet given him. Things you've picked up. Things you've learned, whether I've liked it or not. I need you to be with him, shadow him, to keep him straight."

Here he had paused, not wanting to pick the wrong words, not sure if he had picked the right ones. The look on Little Anthony's face was worse than he'd feared. He had pulled an expression like a boy who had reached into the cookie jar and come out with a mousetrap sprung on his finger.

"Father, I don't need another man in my crew. You know that things are good."

"Ah, that may be. But time may also be short for me. I am an old man. And there are things that are going to have to happen, you'll learn about those soon enough. But the family will survive, and if all goes well, if we've played our cards right, laid our threads into the proper weave, the family will be stronger than it ever has. Ten years from now, whether I'm alive or not, we will be secure. Jake's going to see to that. He knows things you don't know. That is why you need to learn from him."

"I don't need his protection. I don't need him telling me what to do. And you're not going to be doing that either." Here he turned to Jake with accusation for sins not yet committed.

"That's right." Jake paused, then added coolly, the way he would when he was respectful in front of people who didn't know they were related, "Mr. Dolczek. He doesn't need a babysitter. He's been on his own for most of the last five years. He knows what he knows. He's fresher than I am."

"Yes, he's fresher. That's the point. You have the experience. That is what he needs. And you Jake, I thought you had wanted this. I thought you had wanted a chance to be working with the family again."

"Yes, but not," and Jake spread his hands, palm upwards, "like this."

"And what the hell do you mean by that?" Little Anthony was spitting, not sure whether to be indignant at his father for placing a keeper on him like a leash on a dog, or whether to be upset that Jake was back and moving in on his birthright.

Dolczek cleared his throat, and then again, more loudly. "Anthony, please, go downstairs and bring me back a glass of milk. This has been killing me." He cleared his throat again for dramatic effect.

Then, while Anthony rose and left the room, shooting daggers over his shoulder at Jake's back from the always-too-dim hallway, Antonin Dolczek also rose. He walked over to Jake, extended his hand, made him rise, and walked out with him onto the balcony. They stared out at the dark lawn. Its grey green was pure. They stood together and took in the hedges, the trees, the starfield of the city laid out in front of them beyond the walls.

And then Antonin Dolczek said, "I had expected this all to be yours. But it can't be. Not with... not with the boy. I never expected to fall in love, you know. I never expected to marry. By the time you were born I had resigned myself to a life of being old and lonely, except for the company of my nephew."

"You don't have to explain anything to me. I understand the way things… are."

"I know it won't be enough, Jake, but, do you see that care down there? The Packard? The nice, sporty one? That's yours. Anthony thinks it's going to be for him. This is going to hurt him. He's jealous. He's bitter. He's resentful. I think of it as pride. I think of it as him acknowledging his status as my heir. But, when I'm alone at night, just before waking, I know that my son is a petty boy. And I need you to help him become a man. Take the car. It's yours. And he won't say a word about it. It's the one gift I can give you, for now."

"Of course, Anthony's going to need a driver. Part of the role of whoever works as his bodyguard."

"Yes, of course," Dolczek nodded.

"So, maybe he'll take some small pleasure in me having to drive him around in the car that would have been his?"

Still nodding, Dolczek conceded. "There is that. We both know there is that."

Dolczek patted him on the shoulder. This had been the first time, ever, that they had spoken so honestly with each other.

"I won't thank you Jake. I know you won't appreciate it. But I am grateful. Maybe you can be more of a teacher to him than I was a father. And with luck, if plans go well, he will survive, the family will survive. He won't have to ever suffer prison. None of us will. But it's going to depend on you. And you probably won't ever hear another thank you."

"I know. I've grown to accept that."

"I'm afraid you're right."

* * *

Light bulbs flickered in their sockets overhead. Up to that point, from his end, everything was running like clockwork. The truck with the money pulled into the warehouse right on schedule. The reports from the driver and crew were confused, though, about what had gone down. As Dolczek's men began unloading the haul and spreading it between the four cars that would take each portion to a separate drop spot around the city, Marco, the driver, tried to explain.

"It was Jake that told us to go on. We didn't get everything, but we got away clean. Tony wanted us to stay for another load, but they started to argue and Jake waved us on. The cops were coming closer, so we got out of there before they could put a mark on the truck. Jake and them headed off on their own after we left."

"Jake was arguing with Anthony?   About the money?"

Marco looked to the crew from the truck and they all looked away, shrugging their ignorance.

"We're not totally sure, Mr. Dolczek," he said carefully. "Jake was saying we had enough for this haul and that this was just a practice run anyway, for the job next week. But Tony kept acting like he had to go back inside, and that was putting Jake seriously on edge."

Dolczek frowned. He could understand Jake's reasoning. The job was a hit on a small bank on the west side, timed to happen half an hour before the security company had their shift change. The safe in question was the target. It was the same model as the one used in the National Federal's downtown branch, but National Federal was due for a reinstallation of their vault in less than a month. If their man was right, and he could crack the safe in less than fifteen minutes, then he'd be able to crack National Federal's the same before the refit.

But Jake shouldn't have been undermining Anthony's authority in front of Anthony's crew. This kind of thing seemed to have been happening more and more lately and Dolczek was worried. If it kept up, an argument could be made for Anthony's summary judgment of insubordination, family ties notwithstanding. Dolczek was worried for Jake, he knew it could only be a matter of time before his son had had enough, and no matter how right Jake was, no matter how good his advice was, or how much his stubbornness was saving his son grief, the old man feared that blood would be spilled.

Like the laughter of a one-eyed crone at Dolczek's timely thoughts, the squeal of tires was heard in the distance. The roar of the Packard's engine filled the street outside, and the big black car came barreling through the open doors of the warehouse.

It kept on at the angle it entered from, at a speed that was definitely too fast, but suddenly spun to the right, its back end swinging far over to the left as the car ground to a stop. As it whipped around, a shot fired from inside the cab, and then another, the driver's window shattered, and as the glass fell, another shot followed on the echo of the first two. Glass snowflakes tinkled to the cement floor as the car rocked back and forth on its struts.

The large space was filled thick with the shocked silence and the purr of the Packard's engine. In the distance sirens could be heard, but they were moving off in another direction. For now.

The passenger's door opened slightly, and was pushed the rest of the way by the body of Anthony sliding backwards and head first out of the car. The driver's door opened and Jake staggered out and around to grab Anthony by the front of his shirt and drag him out of and away from the car.

Dolczek took steps towards his son, but it was like moving through wet concrete. Sound came to him like he was underwater. Time dilated. It felt like his heartbeats were coming too slowly.

While Dolczek strained against the miles it seemed he had to travel to reach his son's side, Jake opened the rear passenger door where he leaned in and pulled the limp body of a little girl. He placed the child in the front seat and pulled Lorenzo free from the back where he was struggling to climb out. Lorenzo was bloody and breathing hard. He took Jake's assistance with a clasped hand around the forearm, like a warrior saying farewell.

Then Jake was back behind the wheel and the car was in gear, pulling backwards out of the warehouse and away into the night. The roar of the engine filled Dolczek's ears like crashing waves on a rocky beach. His senses shifted from hearing back to vision, as he realized he was cradling his son's head in his arms, that he was on his knees on the dirty cement floor.

Anthony was breathing, shallow, rapid breaths. He has a bloody gash on the side of his head and a hole torn in his shoulder. People were running everywhere now. Men were pulling him up off the floor and tearing Anthony from his arms. He was shouting at everybody to get his boy to the house and to have the doctor there waiting for him. In less than five minutes, the warehouse was empty. Dolczek and his son were in the first car to leave.

Dolczek had Lorenzo put up in one of the spare bedrooms at the mansion so the doctor that came to tend

Little Anthony's injuries would be able to see to them both. Lorenzo passed in and out of consciousness for the next several hours, but would tell him the rest of the story before he died from his wounds.

Dolczek wanted to believe that Little Anthony's gun had discharged accidentally during the skid. He also chose to believe that Anthony had been wounded in a gun battle with the police.

Chapter Fourteen
The Front Door

And that was the last he had seen of Jake. And that was three weeks ago.

The bell rang in the hall to announce that a visitor was at the door. The old man sat up and considered this. The gates were locked, and he was in the mansion, for all he knew, alone. Everyone else was sent out to consolidate their position, trying to get through what was sure to be a hell of a night.

He pushed himself out of the comfortable chair and went to the french doors overlooking the lawn. He scanned what he could of the dark grey expanse, then went out onto the small balcony to look down on the drive. There was only Jake's Packard in its customary place. Tony had claimed it as his, after it was found outside of a hospital on the edge of the Trenches. He paid for the body and glass work and the car had been delivered earlier last week. Anthony wouldn't have pulled the rope for the bell. Dolczek peered down over the edge and couldn't see anyone below on the front steps. The bell rang again.

Going to the desk, he pulled a substantial sidearm from out of the drawers. The revolver was grey and heavy in the moonlight. He checked the clip and deposited it awkwardly in an inside coat pocket as he made his way downstairs.

He put his hand inside the coat, and checked the peephole. No one could be seen through the wide lens set high in the mahogany door.

He opened the door slowly and looked down to meet the gaze of the young boy who stood staring up at the old man and the house that loomed above and beyond him. He was dressed ragged and looked thin, but had a firm-set jaw that belied the nervous way he fingered the envelope he held in both hands in front of himself.

"I was told to give this to the guy who answered the door." He held it up and out, to be taken.

"How did you get in here?" the old man asked as he took the small envelope. It was white, with no name on it, only the capital letter 'D'. He opened it with his index finger hooked under the unglued space on one side and took the piece of stationary out while the boy explained.

"This guy gave me the envelope and told me where to come over the wall to get in. Said I had to take it right away and give it to whoever answered the front door."

But by now Dolczek was reading and had stopped caring about how his mansion's security had been compromised. The letter made it plain. The note read:

Uncle,

>   *Do not blame the boy. I know it is not your style to shoot the messenger, but you must understand that I grabbed him at random from off the street and brought him here. I have paid him a small sum of money to deliver this message at this time. He is, quite possibly the most innocent person you have met today, and for quite some time.*

>   *As much as I have ever wanted to be part of your family you must understand, and hear me now, when I say that I cannot, anymore, do this. I have done terrible things to win your love and I have tried to moralize them, make them grand in scope, think of family. But, I have been pushed too far.*

>   *I am out. I quit. You won't hear from me anymore. I won't bother you anymore. There will be nothing of me, anymore, in this family, in this organization, in this city. All I ask is that I be left in peace.*

>   *And, you will have to also forgive me for what is about to happen. But, there are some trophies that should not be kept.*

>   *I do love you Uncle. Perhaps you will think of me as weak, later, for speaking of love. But if there is to be nothing left to me, I would prefer my legacy be that I thought thoughts of love.*

Giovanni

A bit florid, but that was his nephew, the educated man. It was good to know that those years in college had paid off. The old man looked up from the letter, his face unreadable in creases and shadows. The boy held out his hand expectantly.

"I have been given bad news," the man snarled, "But I have not been driven senseless." Jake's 'innocent' boy had expected to get paid twice. The urchin thrust his hand hard into his pocket and took a step back, when the clock in the hall struck six o'clock.

In the old man's study the grandfather clock also rang out the hour. It stood with its face whitened by the light of a clear moon. Its circuit was bisected by two arrows, long and narrow pointing upwards, short and broad pointing down.

The boy took another step back and was blown forward by the force of the Packard exploding in the driveway. The blast hit on the third ring of the delicate chimes from the entry hall.

He was thrown into the old man, and then pushed off as Dolczek, now with a huge revolver in his hand, spun inside the frame of the doorway. He peered out, after checking the view of the yard from the mirror in the back of the hall. Satisfied, the old man relaxed slightly.

"You'd better go." He looked at the boy hard on the other side of the doorway from him.

The boy peered outside uncertainly as parts of the car settled among the flames smoldering on the lawn.

Dolczek had no time for this. He gave the boy his best evil sneer, "It's not my style to shoot the messenger," he cocked the hammer back on the revolver, "but trespassers are another thing altogether."

The boy took off like a rabbit from the doorway, sprinting for a spot in the hedges west of the main gate. Dolczek took note of this, and would have someone sent to refile the wall spikes in the morning. For now though, he had other phone calls to make.

Chapter Fifteen
A Getaway

A dozen or more blocks away, as sparks from the burning automobile climbed into the evening sky like fireflies on a quest to become distant stars, Jake walked, with his hands in his pockets, making black arrows that pointed to his clean, black shoes. His shadow stretched behind, but it didn't quite reach to three weeks ago, where his thoughts were stalking him.

* * *

The money was going into the back of the truck almost as efficiently as a bucket brigade slinging water towards a raging fire. But, organization was breaking down now. They were at the end stage of their timetable. The money was good, but the real score was the contents of the safety deposit boxes in the front of the cab underneath the driver's seat. The envelopes lodged there contained bearer bonds in the sum of several hundred thousand dollars. They were much more portable, and much more liquid, than the cash in the money sacks that were piling up in the back.

They had hit the bank at 6:30. A quirk in the security timetable had all tellers and executive personnel being out of the building by 6:00, but the night shift for the security team did not arrive until 7:00. This left the bank with a defense force of one guard in the back, near the vault, and one guard in the front, keeping an eye on the lobby. They were a token force left to lock up and turn away customers arriving late. Their presence was a reflection upon the bank management's desire to cut costs and save money rather than protecting it. Jake considered, not for the first time, about the general foolishness of highly educated, well-bred men.

The guard in the front they had gotten the drop on after coming in through the rear and binding and incapacitating the old man in the back. The younger guard in the front had been tied up and locked in the bank president's offices. That was Tony's idea. That was Tony's sense of humor.

They hadn't blindfolded the guards since they were unconscious and the men had entered wearing masks. It wasn't considered, by Tony, to be that much of a problem. Still, Jake would have been happier if they had covered the guards' heads somehow, and gagged them, so that they could move around without the masks. A bit more mobility, a bit more security, and a lot easier to blend into a crowd if they did have to make a rush out the back for some reason.

But at this end stage of the operation, discipline had begun to break down and the masks were coming off anyway. Jake supposed it didn't matter. They were due to be gone in the next ten minutes.

But then they heard the sirens.

There was no guarantee that they were coming for them. But, that was that. You couldn't just hear sirens and ignore them. Not when you're standing in the back alley of a bank with two getaway cars, one filled with cash, and a wide back door, to where you could get to an open vault, and a bound guard. The timetable had changed, and it was time to go. Now.

"Okay, that's it. Last run. We've got enough. Close her up. Get going. We all know where to meet." Jake's orders were quick but calm. He kept his voice low, but let it carry so that everyone knew the score. They had all heard the sirens, and Jake always made sure that there was a Plan B, just in case of contingencies such as this.

The crew was good, and they began switching gears. The last of the masks were off now, stuffed into pockets. Lookouts were at either end of the alley, searching up and down the streets from the shadows.

"Yeah, like he said, get moving. I'll be right back."

Jake called after Tony's retreating back, "We're done." He gestured pointlessly to the Packard. Tony was already inside.

"I said I'll be right back," he called over his shoulder from the hallway inside the bank.

"Go ahead, get in the back of the car. I'll be back in a minute," Jake called over to Lorenzo, Tony's official right hand. Lorenzo 'Lenny' Santorini was smart, seasoned, some would consider him old. This was probably the greatest testament to his wisdom, considering the life he led. "Make sure these guys finish up here. I'm going to pull Tony out from the back."

"Yeah, sure thing Jake. Okay, let's go. You heard the man." And that was that. Lenny was in charge, professional as ever, knowing what to do.

He was a veteran. He'd been through this before. He was cool. Because he had been through this before. He had the rest of Tony's crew being cool now too, because he was calm, giving orders, letting them know exactly what to do and how to do it. He wasn't screaming. He wasn't cursing. He was just telling them the next thing that they needed to do.

That was how things should be done, Jake thought. Not with yelling. Not with braying. Not with bragging. Not with cursing.

Jake left Lenny to it. He went into the bank. From inside he could hear Tony berating the guard. Oh God. Oh God, no. Why had he gone in for 'just one more score'? Why did he have to do this? Why did it have to be like this?

He came down the hallway, towards the wall where the guard was bound, outside the antechamber to the vault. He found Tony there, screaming at the old man.

"Why did you have to open your eyes? Why did you have to wake up? You stupid, stupid, old man. You know. You know this has to be the way it is now."

Tony noticed that the guard looked scared, sad, but was not sobbing. He was probably a grandfather. He had probably been to war.

"Come on, let's go." Jake's mask was still on, but Tony's had been one of the first to come off, not ten minutes earlier. "They're getting closer. Come on, I think they made us."

"Yeah, made us. You're damn right they made us. This pig right here has made us."

Then Tony pulled the trigger. Twice. The guard was dead, two bullets to the chest. Then, one more in the temple, like that mattered. Bile rose in Jake's throat.

"Let's go. Now."

"He made us Jake. I had to do it."

Jake wished that he hadn't been in enough situations like this with Dolczek's son to recognize the way Tony always whined like a kid with his fist caught in the cookie jar, looking for anyone else to blame for him having to break the jar to get his hand out.

"Now. We're leaving *now*."

"Yeah, yeah, just a minute." And he ducked into the vault and came back with one more sack thrown over his shoulder. "Okay, now we can go."

"Just get in the car. I'll clean up here," Jake growled as Tony trotted past.

"Yeah, yeah, you do that."

Jake walked into the vault and looked around. He took out a handkerchief and wiped down anywhere he thought Tony would've laid his hands to take away any evidence of fingerprints. Then he walked back into the hall.

He looked down at the old man, arms tied behind him, rolled over on his side in his own gore. Tony was right. He should have never woken up. He should have never opened his eyes. Jake knelt down, and softly, one eyelid at a time, brought the old man to a countenance of slumber.

"Be at peace old man. I'm sorry. This is never the way it's supposed to be." He could hear the guard upstairs screaming and crying.

There was no time to go upstairs to deal with him. There was no time to go upstairs ad reassure him, to let him know that it was over.

Jake turned the lights out on his way down the hallway. He rounded the corner and closed the door behind him.

It didn't matter. The alarms had already gone off. That was obvious.

The sirens were only within blocks now. The van was gone, thank God. The Packard hadn't moved. The engine wasn't running. Tony was sitting idly in his accustomed place in the passenger's side of the front seat. Lenny was in the back, behind the driver's seat.

Tony was drumming his fingers on the dash, humming to himself, and rocking back and forth, listening to some nameless tune in his head. Jake wondered if it was echoing in there.

He hurried over to the car, got in, slammed the key into the ignition, and drove slowly, hoping they wouldn't get made. When he pulled onto the boulevard everything was clear. So far, so good.

He took it slow, keeping an even speed. He wasn't trying to get anyone's attention. He was two blocks away when the lights swung in behind him. Tony began to tense up, looking over his shoulder again and again.

"Just calm down. Stop doing that. You'll draw attention. We're just three guys out on the town, looking for a good time."

Jake swung right quickly. He had made it half a block before the lights pulled in behind him again. He made a late left turn at the next block and was ready to jog right down an alleyway. But, it was too much.

When the lights of the patrol car came around on them from the corner, following the left hand turn, Tony broke.

"That's it! They've made us. They're following us."

And he did the stupidest, most obvious thing that Tony would have done. He pulled his gun, leaned out the window, and started firing.

Jake drove his foot down on the accelerator like he was crushing a scorpion under his heel. The acceleration jerked Tony around inside the frame of the window.

Lenny was rolling his down, leaning out, and firing in addition. He was firing low, hoping to kick out a tire. That was smart. Killing a cop was never a good idea, especially if they'd begun radioing in the license number of the Packard.

Jake was pulling away steadily. The car had a lot of pick-up.

"Get your ass inside. Roll your windows up." Jake wasn't yelling, but his voice carried the command as it relayed his rage.

The shots began to whizz overhead as the police began to return fire. Lenny grunted and slumped back the rest of the way into the car.

"Lenny? Lenny? Talk to me Lenny."

"It's okay Jake. Just my shoulder. I'll be fine. Everything's okay."

"Yeah, sure, right. Everything's okay. Everything was *going* to be okay." Jake's jaw was tight. His mind was so clouded with rage that he was driving by feel, for all he could see.

"And what the hell's that supposed to mean? You weren't in charge of this job, *I* was."

"That's exactly what I mean. And now we've got one innocent guy dead…"

"No, we've got one security guard dead."

"Right, who didn't need to be. Thanks to you. Thanks to your greedy, stupid… And now Lenny's been hit."

"Yeah? And so what? He's doing his *job*. It's his job to get out there and fire back at them. And what the hell are you doing? You're just driving. You don't give the orders. You don't make the decisions. You work for *me*."

"That's a good point. What the hell am I doing? That's a good God-damned point."

Lenny knew Jake well enough to know when a certain kind of relaxed calm was horribly dangerous, and he just saw it settle on Jake like the Angel of Death. All he could do was grunt his concern while he worked his wounded side into a more comfortable position, and pray.

As the car came over a hill, ripped around a corner, and headed down another small street, closer to a residential neighborhood, the sirens were fading. It seemed like they were losing their tail. And that was good. They were off course, and in neutral territory. But, that wasn't a problem.

Jake slowed down slightly, then reached over and hit Tony as hard as he could, cocking back his right hand and slamming it into Tony's left ear as far as he could. Just once, hard enough to knock Tony's head against the window, which he *had* rolled up.

Tony's mouth moved but no words came out. His lips tried to form a protest, but it was already too late. His thoughts must have been swimming around inside that head, bouncing against that tune from earlier. What was it? Five minutes ago. But nothing was coming out. Nothing worthwhile. Not like it ever did.

Jake swung left with the light. He was doing the speed limit again. He had gone a few more blocks when over the sound of Lenny's heavy breathing that came ragged and indecisive from the back seat, a solid and decisive click came from the passenger's side of the cab. The hammer on Tony's revolver was pulled back, and the gun, he could tell from the edge of his peripheral vision, was aimed at him.

A flex in Jake's wrist brought the derringer into his hand, but his hands were still basically in front of him, on the steering wheel. He couldn't quite get the drop on Tony, even though he was now armed, and then from the backseat, the click of Lenny's hammer being pulled back, was heard. And Jake was sure it was being aimed at Tony. Pretty sure.

Tony was losing it. "Now you listen to me. You pay attention to *me*. I am your boss. I tell you what to do. We do things my way. You don't just sit there and complain about it. You got me? *Look* at me. *Listen* to me."

Tony D, Little Anthony in front of his father, was screaming. He was shaking. It was all Jake could do to glance over at him as they rounded the next corner.

Which is why all he saw was a flash of yellow that registered before the *thump* on the hood and the *crack* on the windshield. And then the second *thump* on the hood as they were slowing down. They were all thrown forward. The small body that had been on the hood was thrown onto the street as the car braked hard.

Lenny's gun went off and blew a hole in the roof over Tony's head. Tony ducked, moved his gun away and pointed it at Lenny. Then, looking wild eyed, not totally aware of what was going on, he let his gun drift aimlessly as he tried to take in what had just happened and what Jake was doing next.

But it didn't matter. The driver's side door was already open and Jake was already around to the front of the car. Jake was kneeling in the middle of the street, over the body of the little girl.

There wasn't anyone around. It was just an empty block, on an empty street, in front of what seemed to be empty houses, facing empty houses. The streetlights were on at the end of the blocks, but nobody else was there.

Why was she here? Why wasn't there anyone else around?
The thoughts kept running through Jake's mind as if they
were trying to run interference to keep him from
processing the information about the red blood stains on
a yellow dress, about the pool of blood under a little girl's
head.

He didn't know if that was from the windshield or
from when she hit the street. There was the faintest
sound, like a whimper, coming from her shallow, ragged
breathing, under broken ribs. He could just make it out
over the sound of the idling motor.

"It's going to be okay. It's going to be okay. It's
going to be okay." He kept saying those five words over
and over again as he smoothed her hair back away from
her eyes. She twitched slightly and looked up at him
before moaning back into a position of relaxed
unconsciousness.

He reached under her. *Why wasn't anybody there?
What was the girl doing in the middle of the street?* He picked
her up and brought her around the passenger's rear door
where Lenny had already opened it for him.

"Here boss, put her in here. She'll be fine. We'll get
her to a hospital. That wasn't your fault Jake. She came
out of nowhere. I don't know where she was coming
from. It was like she was just there, chasing a ball or
something across a street. But, there ain't nobody else out
here. It was just *weird*. She shouldn't've been here Jake.
This wasn't your fault."

"Yeah, yeah, yeah." That's all Jake said.

In his mind he was thinking, *of course she should have
been here. This was her street. This is where she lived. This is where
she was* safe. *This is where she could* play.

But he just said, over and over again, "Yeah, yeah,
yeah," not because he was agreeing with anything Lenny

had to say, but just because all his mind could do was acknowledge that someone else was speaking.

He came around the car again and slid in behind the wheel. Tony was useless and stunned in the front seat. Tony D kept glancing into the back seat. Then at the cracked windshield. Then at Jake. Then at Lenny. Then again at the girl in the backseat. His mouth was moving like when Jake had hit him only a few minutes earlier. And, no words were coming out again, which was good.

As Jake pulled the door closed with his left hand, the derringer, which had been sent home when he had bent to pick the girl up, was back in his hand. And now the muzzle of the small gun was slammed into the bridge of Tony's nose. Jake's arm was straight, and Tony's back was up against the window as the derringer continued to apply pressure to his skull, pinning him there.

"You're right. What the hell am I doing? I'm just driving. Well, that just changed. This is what's going to happen. I'm going to give the orders and you're not going to say *one God-damned word*. Do you hear me? Not *one God-damned word*." With the emphasis he placed on each of the last three words, the muzzle of the gun placed slightly more pressure, for punctuation, on the bridge of Tony D's nose.

He continued, "If you say *one God-damned word* Lenny will shoot you and you will be dead. And we'll say the cops did it. And no one will care. You got me? Not *one God-damned word*."

In the backseat Lenny's face was impassive, not necessarily acknowledging that he had heard what Jake had said, but his eyes were steady, and his gun was pointing at Tony's head also.

"This is my show. *My show*, you got me? What's going to happen is that I'm going to drive us to the warehouse and drop you and Lenny off with your daddy. And then, cousin, I'm going to take this little girl to the hospital so we can hope that there won't be any more death tonight."

His voice took on a stiletto's edge.

"But there might be, do you understand? There might be."

Tony D swallowed to show that he understood. He did not say one God-damned word.

"I'm going to drive now."

And with that, the derringer was gone, back down his sleeve, into its sheath, like magic, the way Jake could do that. And then the car was moving. His hands were back on the wheel. The accelerator was pressed to the floor.

Chapter Sixteen
The Underpass

As I made my way down to the waterfront I had to wind my way through the last of the old business districts. It was in the process of being converted into tracts of condos and apartment blocks crammed into the old counting houses, factors' offices, and import-export businesses with pretty facades and crenellations aplenty to jack the prices up in the crumbling, neglected buildings. After that, I would have to go through a part of the warehouse district, and then a section of land radiating off the old rail yard. And then, I'd be down to the waterfront.

Following the streets made no sense at this point. They were almost always going one way, and almost always going in the wrong direction. When it was present, traffic here was always dangerous for a pedestrian, so it was just as well that I stuck to the alleys and stayed between the buildings along the safer routes I knew.

I slipped through a hole in a chain link fence and entered into an industrial block lit by the lights in fenced-off yards and other loading docks. I tried to avoid looking at any of them.

After I slid between two particularly large hulks of buildings that sat in the night under the orange fog like two resting water beetles towering over me, the alleyway dipped down into a forgotten service passage under a railway track. As I came upon it, the lights under the track winked on in a series, beginning about twenty feet away from me, stretching back into the distance, down, straight, and then up to finish at the other end of the tracks uphill on the other side of the tunnel. In and of itself, this was not particularly disturbing. Lights flickered on and off in this neighborhood all the time. They did it on many nights. They did it just a couple of nights ago when I made my way through here on another walk. But tonight of all nights, I was wary. So as I approached, I made sure to avoid the specific pools of light as I walked past them, coming around the edges, trying not to ruin my night vision by looking into them or through them. I didn't necessarily know what I was trying to avoid seeing, or was trying to make sure I could see, but I just didn't want to step into that light. Not those lights. Not tonight.

Halfway along the ramp down, I stopped. The train was coming and I let it pass overhead, running its full length before I stepped down under the tunnel where the acoustics were sure to have deafened me. Instead I listened to the whale song of the rails as they hummed instrumentally after all the freight had passed over them, like tuning forks, or like the strings off some giant bass fiddle. The humming of the rails rose up and down, rhythmically, singing their own song back to the engineers.

I struck out again, and it was when I reached the bottom of the ramp that I saw her.

I was relieved to actually see her again. I wasn't aware of what had happened following the incident I saw at the loading dock. I wasn't sure she was alive. *Alive? Does that make sense that a hallucination could be alive?* I had seen the man dump a body. I had seen the man shoot at me. But I hadn't seen her since the light blew out. I had to admit to myself that I believed she was alive. But now, seeing her, I *knew* she was alive, at least in whatever timeline was being played out that I was getting these strange glimpses of. And that was good.

What was disturbing, however, was that she was running straight at me.

The lights here formed tight columns in the gloom, being too low to the ground to form proper cones, and they were surprisingly bright for such a derelict area. She skipped through them like the flickering image on a movie screen where the reel was out of time. I could have achieved the same effect with anyone else running past if I had waved my fingers really fast in front of my eyes. And when I considered that, as I saw her appear out of blackness and disappear into shadows, through light, in-out, in-out, there-gone, there-gone, I allowed myself a wry smile, thinking that maybe this was what God was doing to me- wiggling his fingers in front of my eyes.

I had moved further to the side of the passage, backing up o the wall of the tunnel, finding a darker patch to stand in between two of the pillars of light. She didn't look at me. She just ran straight past, making no noise. I could have stepped forward, reached out, and touched her arm, but I turned instead, and watched her go as she moved up the ramp. As she exited the last pool of light she was gone. And that was all. I waited. I looked up and down, both directions, but no other human phantoms emerged.

There was the barest hint of other shadows flowing after her, but they stayed away from me, on the other side of the tunnel. They came and went so quickly I wasn't even sure if I had really sensed them.

I continued on my way, glad that she was alive. I wondered what she was running from, hoping she was running to something instead. I hoped that I would see her again, in the company of the man.

When I reached the top of the ramp coming out from the far side of the service route, the night behind me went dark as all the lights along the passage went out at once.

Typical.

Chapter Seventeen
The Diner

Before Gloria had left the estate that afternoon, she had known that she lived in a Dark City. A life filled with dinner parties and elocution lessons and meeting all the right people had not kept her from knowing that there were dark spaces that filled the city outside the walls that surrounded where she lived.

She only had to look out the window at night to see that the street lights and the headlamps of motorcars pierced a world filled with Dark spaces. She only saw them as gaps in her world, not gaps in her education, not gaps in herself. Just spaces in a void that couldn't be filled. There were things that just weren't there sometimes.

She could never explain this to her father, never explain this sense of incompletion in her perception of the world. It was like there were spaces between spaces. It was like there were gaps within the stitching of reality.

114

She yearned to have them either sewn up, or dig her finger into them, like the worn spot in a sweater.

But in either case, she had to get into the world to do it.

That was something that had never been allowed at home. Despite her cloistered childhood there was one year, not too long ago, where she was taken to see the world. Escorted, practically caged, like the world was a zoo behind the bars of her chaperones and she was seeing it toured past her as she was moved around the globe.

That was when she realized that she lived in a Dark City. Under Mediterranean skies or in the American southwest, there were some cities, she knew, that had stars in the heavens. These cities were wrapped in a tapestry of glory, whether they acknowledged it, recognized it, appreciated it, or not. There were some cities that pulled a blanket of fog over their head on a nightly basis to keep the monsters away behind a white cotton wall. But even these fogbound cities were illuminated in their closed world.

Dark Cities stood in an infinity. They were islands in a bubble. Buildings crowded together for warmth like sheep in a pen. The blackness stretched up to the sky from their alleyways like ebon floodlights.

It was one thing to look from her balcony at night and know she lived in a Dark City. It was another thing altogether to be in it. Now she was swimming in Dark Waters. Now she was running through Dark Streets.

Fog rolled in. Darkness grew. And shadows danced. She prayed the last was her imagination.

But she kept moving anyway.

She made the best time she could, running in heels. *God damn that man.* Jake, he said his name was, for making her run in heels. Couldn't he have gotten a car? Couldn't he have hailed a taxi? It wouldn't have done any good. Could they have trusted any driver?

So she turned right when she thought she was supposed to turn right and turned left when she thought she was supposed to turn left. She made the best time she could, kept heading downhill, like he said.

She ran through pools of lamplight that were laid out across the street like pearls on a string. She kept to the bigger streets, avoiding the dark alleys, remembering the dancing shadows of her imagination. And when she finally reached the street she was supposed to reach, she looked around and found that she was only a block away from her destination.

It was an out of the way diner on the edge of the waterfront. Jake told her to look for the sign that said Greasy's. It was a pool of white light in a Dark City.

There was something about Dark Cities. It seemed like the lights of the buildings, whether they were candles at dinner, the overhead lamps in a library, or the pools of light in a foyer of a hotel, nothing seemed quite bright enough in a Dark City.

Except for places like this, places she had never been. And the way it pushed back the darkness was welcome. She could smell pie by the time she had reached the parking lot. She knew she could taste coffee just by walking through the door. This place was safe. It was indeed, an island, in a world she had not yet learned to know.

Gloria considered the outside of the… establishment, with dubious caution. She wasn't dressed for this place. She wasn't dressed for this neighborhood, come to think of it. The sign flickered neon reds on the rooftop over the harsh yellow light that came from the large glass windows on three sides of the building. The diner seemed to clamp down on its lot like some mussel washed up into the night from the waves at the docks below, sole survivor of a forgotten storm. She squared her shoulders and went in, aiming for the one employee she could see, a ridiculously large man with his back to the door, working the grill behind the counter.

Jake knew when he sent her here what kind of place Greasy's was. Greasy's was not the kind of place you would find in the phone book. For one thing, it wouldn't file properly under Restaurant or Fine Dining. One lunch counter and a string of booths lining walls under the windows were all that passed for seating. The owner wouldn't want to list it under any category that it would fit in, assuming the phone company would include those categories in its noble publication.

For another thing, anyone that would've ever eaten there knew that it wasn't the kind of place that you went if you had to look up where it was, or call to get directions. For that matter, Jake wasn't even sure if the place had a phone.

No, check that. There was *a* phone, a pay phone. But Jake was pretty sure that the only time it was ever used was to call the fire department. It was a well-known fact among the resident patrons that the grease-trap installed under the grill, typically dormant, would annually erupt into a small, containable, but highly entertaining grease fire.

The owner would allow this to happen, whichever owner happened to be in charge at the time, because it was also a well known fact that after the annual eruptions of what the locals began to refer to as Little Old Faithful, crowds of people would come by to see what damage had been done that time. And usually, they would stay for pie.

There was no evidence of recent fire damage that Gloria saw as she entered. All the evidence was of older, more venerable, fire damage.

"Yeah?"   The ox working the grill somehow indicated her without turning around. He flipped some things that sizzled when they landed, then looked over his shoulder at her, cocking an eyebrow.

"Are you Greasy?"

The cook spat, hitting the grill, where his contempt went up in a puff of oiled steam. "I washed my hands, if that's what you're asking. What? Is this a joke? Ain't no Greasy. Sign's busted. Just reads GREASY S. Name stuck."   He scrubbed at some grill droppings with the edge of his spatula. "You want something or what?"

She eyed the space behind the counter. Considering the grill that had been so recently vented on by the surly cook, she decided to stick to something that hadn't been spit at recently, probably. "Coffee will be fine, thank you."

"Suit yourself. You sitting down or what?"

She glanced around, registering the layout of the diner in a way she hadn't when taking its census earlier. She nodded to the cook, who was looking over his shoulder at her again, and moved off to a booth in the corner with its back to a wall and a view of the door.

From out of a swinging door, a waitress swept in and made eye contact with the cook after passing her eyes over Gloria. With some silent signal, she moved to the coffee pot and poured a mug for the woman in the evening gown sitting in the last booth.

"You want some pie sweetie?" she said, putting the mug in front of the blonde. In the background, the phone rang and the cook answered it gruffly.

"No, thank you. I'm not really hungry."

"Best pie in the city."

"I'm sure it is. It's just been a long night."

"Tell me about it. My feet are killing me."

"Try running in heels through the waterfront."

"Not if you paid me."

The women smiled at each other.

"Suit yourself then." Her head turned toward the back door. "I'll be right back. I have to check on something." She paused, considering the young woman in the evening gown sitting at her booth. "You sure you're okay sweetie?"

"I'm fine. Really. Thanks. I'm supposed to be meeting someone here."

This got Gloria another "Suit yourself." The waitress, Gladys, her nametag had read, slipped a glance at the cook and pushed her way back into the rear rooms of the diner concealed behind the swinging door.

Gloria's thoughts returned to black swirls of shadow, dark memories, and steaming coffee.

"You really should have tried the pie. Best in the city."

Her head shot up from where it was considering the black depths of the mug ringed in her two hands, as Jake slid into the booth across from her. The soft *whup whup* of the swinging door behind her answered the question about where he had come from. She looked over her shoulder at where the cook was standing at the grill, eyes fixed on the couple in the booth. She brought her eyes back to the man in the rumpled black suit.

"You look terrible…"

"Jake," he reminded her. "Thanks. You're beautiful, by the way."

And she blushed as he smiled that damned smile.

"Are you okay?"

He stretched a little, as if checking to be sure, and then conceded, "Yeah, I'm okay."

He had scanned the room when he came in, but now the cook had his full attention. Jake had seen the behemoth trudging towards them from his spot at the end of the grill, but he had been so caught up in Gloria that it didn't register until the massive shadow fell across the table.

The spatula, which was held in his right hand, might as well have been a butcher's knife with all the intensity with which the cook held it.

"You, I need to talk to. Right now." A sideways glance to the right with one eyeball pinned Gloria to her seat. "You, stay."

With that, he reached over with a left hand the size of a frying pan and lifted Jake out of the booth by the front of his jacket. He half led, half dragged Jake to the end of the counter where he sat him down on one stool and spun him around to face the grill.

Even though he walked the full length back to the end of the counter before returning to face him, Jake did not move. He wouldn't've. He knew that if he had tried to make a break for it before the large man passed the door he would have been caught up in one of those massive gorilla arms. Then the bruiser was too close to Gloria for Jake to risk a break for it. Then finally, with the monster behind the counter again and within reach, Jake knew that he wouldn't have been able to move from the seat without one of those tree trunks shooting out and grabbing him by the back of his jacket, and his shirt, and maybe part of his neck, and the top of his head. Jake became resigned to the fact that he had nowhere to go and no time to get there.

The cook's frame filled Jake's world as he stood in front of him across the counter and leaned down on his knuckles to speak quietly to his customer. "My brother is dead, and you know something about it. Don't lie."

Jake couldn't figure what this was about, so he stalled. "You'll have to be more specific buddy. It's been a long night." Then it hit him.

The beady eyes, the lantern jaw, the lack of neck, the hairy arms. *Oh god.* "Oh God, you're…"

"Yes. I think you called him Mook. Most people did. You will explain to me how he died. Be specific. Don't lie." The words were slow, controlled, and deliberate. They seemed to come with great effort, like the slow turning of a millstone. Whether this was from mental or emotional strain, Jake couldn't tell.

Jake glanced over at Gloria who was staring at both of them. She hadn't heard a word of the conversation, but she sat tensed, ready to move, but not knowing where, how, or when. The slightest slide of his chin sent a subtle 'no'. This was enough to make her stay put. But she did not relax.

He looked back at the cook, met his eyes and held his gaze. Gladys was still in the back. He said, "Okay. I'll tell you the truth. You know your brother ran with a rough crowd." Jake didn't know if that was true or not, but figured he should establish something neutral that would still provide context. "I ran into the crew he worked for. You see that lady over there? Well, this is what I saw…"

And Jake told him the whole thing. He walked him through it from the time he met her at the bar to the time they made it out of the storeroom. He explained how he came into the storeroom, shot out the light, how he saved Gloria, and how he killed Mook.

"I appreciate your honesty." Jake was certain that 'appreciate' was probably the most multisyllabic word the cook had said in recent memory, but he did not comment. He did not want to risk anything. The cook's features seemed undecided.

Then, "My brother... was my brother. And I loved him." The words came slowly, like the sun through a cloudy dawn. "But you're right. My brother was not good. But that's not going to stop our mother from crying tonight. Now tell me again. You shot him, right?"

"Yes."

The cook seemed to grow hard again, losing any softness he had gain by mentioning his mother. The large man sighed, resigned. "I had you down for bare hands in a month with an 'r' in it." He turned his head and spat, and missed the grill. Jake realized that he hit the mouse which ran for cover, out of sight. Jake swallowed as he saw the shadow of the mouse follow the fleeing rodent a second after the mouse ran away.

"You'll... have to talk to Cheese about that."

The cook spat again, hitting the grill this time, expressing what he likely thought of Cheese and his recent fortune. A puff of steam geysered up.

"Um, are we done?"

"Yeah, we're done. I appreciate your honesty." The cook turned his massive frame back to the grill in slow, mechanical movements.

Jake slowly turned his stool to get up, his hands remaining flat on the counter until he stepped away. He slowly walked back to the booth, never taking his eyes off of the cook. He finally slid into the seat opposite Gloria.

Gladys came out of the back, looked at the two of them, looked over at the cook who was hunched over the grill, looking a little smaller than he did before, working.

Jake brought his eyes back to Gloria as Gladys walked over to the large man, and put her hand on his right shoulder, tears showing. She looked as if she knew something, as if she knew what was going on, and how to help. He kept working, ignoring her. But she stood there for a long while, watching him, while the two at the booth continued to talk.

"So here's our situation. I have so far tonight killed at least three men, one of whom is Antonin Dolczek's son. I'm out of ammunition, friends, and am not even sure if we have passage out of town. We're supposed to meet my contact around eleven at the docks. If we all make it there, then we're home free. If not, we're all dead."

Gloria's face was in shock. "Tony's dead?" Her voice was only a whisper.

Jake blinked, and then inquired slowly, "You know Tony D?"

Gloria looked down into her coffee and whispered again. "He was my fiancé. I think maybe it's time for that talk."

"Yeah... I think so." Jake's heart was beating slow. Like an elephant's. Like a coronary.

"My name is Angelina Gloria Turino."

"Oh shit."

"Wait, it gets better."

"No, no, no," Jake moaned and rubbed the palm of his hand down his face, wiping his eyes dry.

"Oh yes, but wait till you hear about the wedding that didn't happen today."

"Wedding? Today?" he asked weakly.

"This afternoon I was to become Mrs. Anthony Jonathan Dolczek. But now I'm not. Of Course."

"No, no, no, shit no, shit no, shit shit shit, noooo."

"Don't swear dear. There are ladies present." She was smiling, a little. It must have been out of pity. If it were Jake smiling at Jake it would have been out of pity.

"Oh God."

"Better. Anyway, yeah, we were supposed to marry today. Almost nobody knew about it. You can't advertise that sort of thing. Can you imagine what it would be like having your wedding crashed by a rival family's herd of gunmen? Probably not, but it was a consideration. A girl has to be on top of things like that. But I was saying; I've known Tony for a few years, but I didn't love him. It was our fathers' idea. The plan was that we'd join the families and then their organizations would control half the city between them." She paused before shooting forward in one last breathless rush.

"I couldn't do it. Something in me just snapped and I couldn't be that bird in the gilded cage anymore. You know? Maybe you don't know. Anyway, I packed a bag and flagged a cab and was gone. I stopped at Monty's, my bag is still there, Christ, I checked it with the coat girl, and changed to fit in while I figured out where to go. Then it got weird. Oh, and I met you, too."

Her hand left the coffee cup and patted his limp left hand. His right still covered his face in a splayed-fingered sign of slumped exhaustion. One eye peaked out at her.

"I think we're done talking now."

Chapter Eighteen
The Greasy Spoo

"More pie sweetie?"

Ed was working the counter, and Gladys was at my booth.

"Gladys, you're an angel. An angel with pie."

She snorted, but her upturned nose didn't put me off. Despite the lines in her face you could see the beauty Gladys had always been. And if she wasn't older than my grandma, I was tempted to follow through with my mother's advice. But, I could tell, by the ring that had welded itself to her finger, and by the way she never quite met the eyes of the men who still stared after her, I could tell, that she carried pie home to some other man at the end of the day. Sigh.

Just as well. I took a moment to begrudge the decades and the circumstances of her marriage that kept us apart.

"No, not tonight. I guess I should be going. I don't know."

"Well make up your mind sweetie, I'm getting off. The new girl's coming on in a few minutes."

"How about another cup of coffee then? Maybe I'll stay."

"Suit yourself. I'll let you settle up with her."

The new girl was pretty, and I decided to have another slice of French Silk to follow my third cup of coffee. I stayed for another half hour. We talked for a bit. She was nice.

But then I had to keep moving. So, I settled up. I left an extra tip, making sure she would share it with Gladys. She said she would, and asked me to come back soon.

I swung left after leaving The Spoo and headed towards the docks. Invariably, no matter where I took myself on these walks, if I was out long enough that was where I'd end up. If I ever hoped to get to bed.

You'd think I'd stay inside the diner for the famous pie and the bright lights. Or find some all night coffee shop, or someplace where I could find nothing but neon, or sound, or some other sensory distraction. But I was always pulled to the docks.

Downhill, downhill, to the sea. Out onto the wharf, out onto the pier. If you go far enough out, and turn the right direction, if you get all the way to the end, and position yourself just a little bit to the right of center as you face out to the ocean, you can't see the land to either side. All you have is an unobstructed view of the black.

Chaos above, chaos below. Sometimes there's stars reflected in the water as they blaze overhead. Sometimes there's a band of half-light drawn out of the city lights that runs through the fog that races across the horizon like St. Elmo's dawn. But these serve only to accent the emptiness, to dress it, to define it, to plumb its depths and let you know that it is eternal.

And I'll stare. And I'll stare out into the night. And when I can't take it anymore, that's when I'll turn my back on the black. And then, as far out as you can get out on the land, sticking out onto that pier into the water, with the sky above and the ocean behind, I face the world.

Blazing lights crawling uphill into the sky, looming over, almost curving over, its own breaking wave ready to come down on top of me. And I have a choice standing there, on the edge: to step back into the black, or walk forward, and face my fear, for one more night.

Every little light casts a shadow. And I could either succumb to all of the black behind, or face the little terrors that every open window, that every streetlight, that every moon shadow casts in the middle of the city. Cars and trucks chase through the streets, their headlights throwing shadows in front, and pulling them behind. Helicopters roam the night like fireflies. Searchlights stab up into the sky intermittently, advertising this or that, drawing attention to the piece of night that they're fighting back, that they're pulling people towards. A rainbow of sparks, yellows and blues and reds, neons, and argons.

And I cannot decide if it is greater or more terrible than all of the emptiness behind me.

This creates, no, forces, clarity for me. I am caught in the balance of a series of parities as I stand on the edge: Do I walk into the light that scares me? Can I stare into the black any longer? Do I step backwards into it and end it all? Do I stand with my back to the light and try to deny it? Ultimately the decision has to be made.

And it is, always the same, as I walk home, having gone to the edge, again. And returned.

Chapter Nineteen
The Pool Of Lamplight

They were maybe ten blocks from the piers when the call came from behind them. At first it seemed like some wordless croaking of a seabird in the night, but the hard edge resolved into the cry of a name.

"Jake!"

The couple had followed all the alleys they could, but there was nothing but straight street leading down to the docks from here and they had to break into the open. They had been making good time on foot and figured they were home free. The harbor was in sight below at the end of a pearl string of streetlights that led down the hill.

They stopped in a pool of lamplight and Jake held Gloria close as they turned and face the advancing men. They had been nailed clean, with no obvious escape routes, no ammunition, no way out.

The crowd of men drew together from over a couple of blocks into the street. The trap was flawless.

They must have had spotters on the roofs, Jake thought to himself, signaling what men they could into position once the couple was spotted. Three intersections back, Dolczek's car was parked in the middle of the street, and the old man himself was moving in the nucleus of the knot of men. It was his voice that had brought them to a halt, his command that drew the noose tight.

Jake held Gloria with his left arm around her waist, pulling as much of her behind him as he could manage. They took a step back as the men drew up to the edge of the pool of lamplight. They made way for Dolczek who took stage front and center. In the distance a cat roused the attention of a group of fenced dogs, and from the sounds of it one of them got lucky, because the cat screamed before noisily clearing their territory.

Sometimes ironic symbolism really pissed Jake off. He held Gloria closer still.

A warm wind picked up from behind the couple and plucked at their clothes as it ruffled the brims of the hats of the men facing them. A few of Dolczek's men, men Jake had worked with and counted as family, had their guns pulled and trained on the couple.

Dolczek cleared his throat, and squared his slumped shoulders.

"You have no idea the pain I have suffered today."

"I'm sorry Mr. Dolczek. This isn't all that it looks like."

"It is exactly what it seems. My most trusted man has, by all accounts, broken up the peace talks with Turino. And now we find him in the arms of Turino's own daughter, on the night she left my son at the altar."

"I swear to you Mr. Dolczek, I only met Gloria tonight. We're both on our way out. Please, just let us go."

Jake's head swam. Why wasn't Dolczek saying anything about Tony? He knew Lenny must have explained what had happened that night three weeks ago. Had Dolczek found out about what had happened to Tony D in the tunnel? Maybe the old man just couldn't bring himself to put shape to the tragedy by invoking it.

"You know I can't do that Jake. But for what has happened with Tony I could have looked over any other one thing. But Jake, you know how it is." His voice was low, quiet, with a calm that overrode all the emotion lying below the next elevation in volume. Jake and Gloria took another step back.

Behind them, and to the side, apparently invisible to the mobsters, swam a school of shadows. They were never in direct line of sight, but present for sure in the way the night crowded just a little bit tighter around the light. The warm wind blew a little stronger.

Dolczek continued. "Ms. Turino, I almost believe I know why you did what you did. And," he shook his head, "I almost could have applauded you for the effort. But sadly, things have progressed beyond any one of us. I'm sorry Ms. Turino, but my men never found you tonight. Jake was never here. You and my son were seen booking passage at the port and have eloped despite my and your father's wishes for a public wedding. With luck, Benito will accept that." Dolczek sighed heavily, as if ashamed of his own words. He looked down, as if in contrite prayer.

It sunk in. Jake pieced it together. Dolczek would salvage the peace and consolidate his empire with Turino after all. He would also have his revenge, taking Turino's daughter as private payment for circumstances that took his son. He wasn't talking about Tony's death because it wasn't common knowledge. And likely wouldn't be. If

Dolczek succeeded in offing Gloria then he could pass off the elopement story and the organizations could continue their merger while the parents grieved in silence, at least one of them maybe never really knowing what had happened to their child.

These were the moments when ice ran down Jakes back. He had faced evil men who meant to kill him before. He had killed many of them for trying. But when Dolczek turned off his humanity like this, that's when Jake realized fear. No small or instinctive part of his brain could ever dictate an action to cut through a confrontation with Dolczek when he was being ruthless.

Jake took one more step back and felt the soft pressure of darkness behind him. He looked and saw his heel at the edge of the lamplight. More of Dolczek's men were drawing their guns. Gloria gripped him tighter and whispered in his ear.

"I see them too. Jake, I don't know about you, but I'd rather live free in hell than die a slave in heaven."

Jake nodded. That pretty much had been what it had been all about, summed up right here at the end.

The wind and the shadows pressed against his back, buffering him and Gloria, but also somehow pulling them. Behind him shapes lived in a deeper darkness beyond obvious space and time. In front of him men who were simply men prepared a certain death as they took aim.

Then Dolczek spoke, lifting his head, his whisper carrying through the night.

"I love you too, Giovanni."

In the heartbeat between whispered words and the pulling of a dozen triggers, Jake and Gloria stepped backwards, together, into the unknown darkness where shadows hunted unknown prey.

Chapter Twenty
The End Of The Road

It was the sound of a cat screaming that made me turn around. As I looked over my shoulder, a garbage can fell over about half a block back. A dark shape, only a cat, ran off, down into an alley. But, as I lifted my eyes upward and down the sidewalk, a streetlamp about three lights down, that had been out, hummed, flickered, and then snapped on.

And there they were.

A warm wind picked up and started growing stronger. It was hot, strange, like from a furnace, or the breath of the sun. It tugged at the back of my legs. It made my windbreaker billow forward into strange balloons off of my stomach and under my armpits. Most amazingly, it tugged at the hem of her gown, and plucked at the edge of his jacket.

Their backs were to me, and I could see his left arm curled around her waist, pulling her towards him. They stood hip to hip as they faced the group of men who stepped out of the shadows to be visible through the cone of dirty yellow light.

The immediate relief I felt at seeing the two for them together was caught and stuffed back inside. Had they found each other only to be brought down like dogs in the street? At least two of the thugs in the crowd facing off with the couple were carrying guns, drawn. I'm sure they weren't the only ones.

These men were also dressed in outdated clothing, and they ranged in age from the fresh-faced teenager to the obviously old. The oldest of them stood in the middle. I got a clearer look at him and realized he wasn't so much old, as he was perceptibly tired. His face was folded with experience, and creased by the weight of years come too fast.

And while the old man spoke, leading his men in confrontation with the man and the woman, I could see a sadness in his eyes, as if he had just been stabbed. There was a sorrow that pressed on his shoulders, and a loss, a burden of grief that extended beyond some more recent pain, going back, stretching behind him, into the past.

His mouth formed angry words under those sad eyes, but he didn't seem to raise his voice. As before, I couldn't hear anything that was said by these phantoms, any noise at all from the light, but I was nonetheless held by what was being played out in front of me.

He stopped talking. The man and the woman stepped backwards towards the edge of the light, towards me. The old man said something else in reply to something that must have been said by one of the couple. Then he frowned, tragically. This was not an expression of anger or displeasure, but more sadness. And then he shook his head. He looked down, not meeting their eyes, then looked up again. He spoke two or three words. Then all of the men, those not already drawing a bead on the man and the woman, started reaching into their jackets and drawing their side arms, aiming them at the couple.

The pair took another step back and then hesitated. The woman looked at the man, and then whispered something. He set his jaw, looked slightly over his shoulder, saw that the heel of his shoe was just at the edge of the pool of light, and then, pulling her tightly to him, he stepped them back, out of the light, backwards, onto the street in front of me.

The wind, which had been growing in strength, unleashed as if a door slightly ajar had been kicked wide open. The rush of the hot wind that had been pressing fog up and up into the city cleared the night sky and made the stars overhead look down like the sparkling heartbeats of angels. Shadows ran past me with the wind at their backs.

They swarmed. They flowed. They swept along the ground. They leapt past my shoulders, over my head, dancing past me, streaming past the couple. All of them funneled into the light, and then out and into the men.

The gunshots fired, I saw flashes. Hands jerked, and arms leapt back as mouths opened in screams, exclamations, grunts. Whenever a bullet struck a shadow it did not pass through. As intangible as the shadows may have seemed, nothing went past them. Yet they held the touch of anger as they struck back.

They tore into the men, literally, and I was grateful that the glimpses I had were only just that, as the shadows swarmed over them, fell upon them, crashed upon them like breaking waves. They drove the men back, out of my view, out of the light, and under the weight of their streaming mass.

Having already been shot at tonight, I couldn't have said whether the shield of phantoms was even necessary, if the bullets would have been able to come out of the light at the couple, or past them to me.

The man and the woman stayed there, in front of the light, in front of me. He held her close, shielding her. The headlight of a car washed over them, a gentle shower of white light. And as it rode up the silver lines of her dress, it set silver highlights afire in her hair, it caught the glint of a gold ring on his right hand, it caught the whites of his eyes as he looked down at her, promising her, holding her, keeping her safe. The light passed, and they were gone. Their silhouettes no longer stood between me and the light.

And past the pool of light, past the street lamp that had flickered on a minute earlier, I saw nothing. There were no shadows, no mobsters. And then, as I reconciled this, the light flickered again, and went out, as if a switch had been flipped somewhere in heaven, and the connection had been cut.

Chapter Twenty One
The Docks

Cheese met them at the head of the wharf. Jake didn't ask how he got there ahead of them and didn't want to know how he managed to secure the two pieces of luggage that he had in tow.

"I stopped by your place Jocko. Grabbed a few things. Called in a few favors from some friends of mine so I could get some things for the lady. Had to guess at the size. Sorry miss, hope you understand. Hope they're the right fit."

She smiled at the funny little man with the pointy nose, and said, "I'm sure they'll be fine."

He smiled back. "I'll probably never meet you again, ma'am. Just wanted to let you know that if Jake says you're okay, then you're okay. It's been a pleasure." Which for Cheese, was saying a lot.

Her smile twinkled. And then, impulsively, she leaned down and kissed him on the cheek. Cheese smiled wider than Jake had ever seen him smile before, and imagined it was as wide as he would ever smile again. And, goddamnit, Cheese blushed. There's something Jake never thought he'd see till the end of his days, even after a night like this. The little man with the pointy nose blushed. *Ha,* Jake thought, *there is a God.*

Jake and Cheese shook hands. Then Jake shouldered the bags and walked along, with his lady, to Pier 8.

They stopped under a light rigged up on a tall pole near the freighter's gangplank. He set the bags down. She looked up at him.

"This is it?"

"Yes. This is it. Done. We've made it. We're going to make it."

And with that he pulled her to him and kissed her. He had kissed her before, in the tunnel under the nightclub, but this was different. He kissed her the way a man should kiss a woman. He kissed her with absolute promise of a life together. His kiss was safety. His kiss was love. They separated and, goddamnit he couldn't help it, he blushed. She smiled and hugged him tighter.

He squeezed her shoulders tight, and just over her head, he caught movement in the shadows. Then he relaxed as he saw the shadows take a more solid shape, something he could actually recognize. They weren't shadows at all, but the silhouette of a boy hiding in the shadows.

He let her step back a little and waved the boy over. "C'mere. Yeah you, c'mere you little bastard. You again? Well, c'mere, I've got another job for you. You think you'd like to earn another dollar? These bags, right here, up to the passengers' cabin. The captain or one of his crew will tell you where to put them. Tell'm you're with us. They'll tell you where to store the bags."

"Well... well thanks, mister. What makes you think I'm not going to just run off with them?"

"You don't strike me as a thief, and I know criminals. And where could you go? You've got all of ten feet between here and the gangplank. Once you get on the ship, take them to the stateroom the crew tells you to. That's all you've got to do. Here's the dollar." The boy took the money, shouldered the bags, and was on his way up the gangplank.

"Are you sure about that?" She looked up at him, arms still around his waist.

"What's the harm? He could use the money. What's he doing hanging around the docks in the middle of the night? Obviously he could use the money. And besides, I wanted to just stand here and look into your eyes, just a little longer."

He smiled that damned smile. She smiled back and hugged him close again. Everything was going to be all right. She knew, because his kiss had made a promise.

Chapter Twenty Two
The Docks

I turned right and headed down the length of the pier. I walked straight, down the middle of its width, towards the end, towards the open sea. Moving straight down the middle like this I avoided all the lights that pooled intermittently from side to side, cast from flood lights rigged at intervals alternating along its length.

Ahead of me black sea met black sky, and the not-quite-dawn rolled like an angry haze from right to left, crashing against the city lights where the land curved out of the harbor and back north up the coast. Here and there, a bell rang on a buoy. Water slapped against the pilings of the pier. Ships creaked at other docks. I was halfway down the pier when I saw them for the last time.

They were in a pool of light, on the left, third from the end. I could see them clearly, a man and a woman, her still in her silver gown, him in a very rumpled business suit. But them, for sure, *the* man and *the* woman, holding each other. He leaned down and kissed her. It was a kiss that promised. A kiss that spoke of a life together somewhere else. Away from men with guns. Away from being chased. Away from the shadows, the shadows of their past.

Behind them, through the cone of light, I could clearly make out the ship that waited, its gangplank extended to where it would hit the pier, if it were actually there. I turned my back to give them privacy.

When I looked again, they were gone. There was no ship past the light.

But what I could see, if this can be expressed clearly, was a brighter night. It was a night that did not hang with darkness, but was simply wrapped in the stars, in the moon, in the wind, in the distant fog.

These two had gone. The shadows had gone. It all seemed to have gone. Either up a gangplank, or out of my head, or across the sea, or into the depths of time. I don't know.

I walked to the end of the pier and I stared for a long, long time listening to the bells of the buoys, the water slapping against the pilings, and the creak of the ships. Everything else remained constant.

And, when I turned around, it wasn't just through the lights that I saw how the shadows had gone. Dawn was still hours away, but everything was cleaner. There was no sense of pursuit. There was no sense of terror. If anything, there was a calm, clean, whisper of hope, of love, of promise.

I headed home; no longer afraid of the darkness, because I knew angels stalked the shadows for even... darker... things.

The End

I don't know exactly what I saw that night. Or, to be precise, I can't explain it. But, I do know that a man loved a woman. And he fought for her, and she fought for him. And something else fought for them. Maybe it was love that saw them through.

Maybe I would never know a love like that. Maybe this was a promise that would never come to me. But somehow it was nicer to know, in the course of one evening, to be shown, not in a movie or off of a dime store romance rack, that this was real. I had *seen* it. That made it real.

That was enough for me to get on with the next day. That was enough for me to go to bed tired the next night. That was enough for me to dream about. Without any fear. With only hope. And maybe, a little promise.

ABOUT THE AUTHOR

Robert J. Schulenburg is a native of San Jose, California. His career in Special Education has led him to serve in Central America and the Caribbean with the US Peace Corps. His study of culture, myth, and religion from around the world has heavily influenced his writing, prompting studies in how the condition of the individual influences and is influenced by the strange world we all live in.

You may send any correspondence for Robert to:

authors@samestrangeworld.com